NOV 2017

Paper Cranes

A Fairytale Twist Novel

Jordan Ford

COVINGTON PUBLIC LIBRARY
622 5TH STREET
COVINGTON, IN 47932-1137

© Copyright 2017 Jordan Ford
www.jordanfordbooks.com

*****

All rights reserved. This book or any portion thereof may not be reproduced or used in any manner whatsoever without the express written permission of the author.
This is a work of fiction. Names, places, businesses, characters and incidents are either the product of the author's imagination or are used in a fictitious manner. Any resemblance to actual persons, living or dead, actual events or locales is purely coincidental.

*****

Cover art (copyright) by Dwell Design & Press.
http://parchmentplace.wixsite.com/dwell-design

*****

ISBN: 1548049182
ISBN-13: 978-158049188

For lovers of Rapunzel

I grew up on fairytales. They fed my romantic heart, fueled my imagination, and made me believe in the impossible. Even though Paper Cranes is written as a real-life story with a fairytale twist, it was inspired by my all-time favorite—Rapunzel. So if you've always dreamed of a handsome prince climbing a tower to rescue you...then this story is written for you.

xx

Once upon a time there was a boy who was lost.

He had no compass, no map, and he couldn't find his way home. He wandered the world in aimless despair...until one day he discovered a tower and decided to climb it.

JORDAN FORD

1

The Lost Boy

"Tristan! Hey, Tristan! Wait up."

Stepping to the side of the corridor, Tristan glanced over his shoulder. Mikayla Oswald was bouncing up behind him, her petite body insignificant against the backdrop of bustling students. She could easily pass as a middle schooler yet was a junior, just like him.

Part of him wanted to pick up his pace and duck around the corner before she could reach him, but manners had him slowing to a stop and waiting for his enthusiastic helper.

"Hey." She hugged her binder to her chest as she caught up to him, tapping her finger against the thick spine. Her button nose wrinkled when she smiled, squishing the freckles on her pale face and reminding Tristan of a hamster.

He pushed the thought from his mind, forcing a grin, which probably looked as half-assed as it felt.

"Hi." He nodded, then glanced past her shoulder. He wasn't really sure what she was hoping for and thought minimal eye contact would be for the best.

"It's Mikayla." She pointed at herself.

"Yeah, I remember." Tristan adjusted the beanie on his head and shoved his hand in his pocket.

She grinned and tucked a loose lock of mousy brown hair behind her ear. "I, um, was just wondering where you were going."

"Class." He flicked his thumb over his shoulder.

"Oh, okay, because I thought you had English now and it's that way."

Tristan followed her pointer finger and shut his mouth against the curse he wanted to mutter.

Instead, he cleared his throat and turned back the way he'd come. "Right."

The hum of student chatter buzzed around him, noisy and irritating. He shifted sideways and began to move through the crowd but was stopped by a tug on his sleeve. He rolled his eyes and clenched his jaw while Mikayla squeezed past a group of freshmen and stepped up beside him again.

"You know, our lockers are right next to each other so

if you want to meet me in the morning before school, I'm happy to show you around. I mean, I've kind of been asked to do that anyway and you've been here like two weeks already, so...well, are you going to let me? You know, help you?"

"I'm good." Tristan's voice sounded flat, the way it always did, but he wasn't sure how to change that. He mustered a closed-mouth smile—all he could manage—and picked up his pace, heading away from the only student at Burlington High that had taken the time to try to befriend him. Although, she had been assigned the task.

Either way, he wasn't interested.

Mikayla's crestfallen expression nibbled at his conscience, but he didn't want to encourage her. He wasn't there to make friends, and he definitely didn't need a curious, overenthusiastic pip-squeak following him around. She'd only ask questions, and then the story would come out.

The pathetic, demeaning story that he was still caught inside of. Like an overused bookmark, tattered and torn, he was trapped within the pages of a tragedy he never saw coming.

A tragedy that seemed to have no end.

2

The Pointless Tragedy

Miss Warren was already speaking when Tristan slipped into class. Her pale brown gaze brushed over him, her perfect features flashing with an acute smile before turning back to the whiteboard. She was nice enough not to lecture him in front of everybody, and he quietly sat down while she wrote up the name of the play they'd be studying over the next few weeks.

Romeo and Juliet by William Shakespeare

Tristan suppressed his groan, settling for an eye roll instead. Why were teachers obsessed with that play? Why study such a depressing run of events that could have so easily been avoided?

In Tristan's opinion, the biggest tragedy was the fact that it had stood the test of time. It was constantly being regurgitated and remade just so people could fall in love and then have their hearts torn out of their chests and stomped on. He pictured his mother sniffling at the television, dabbing at her eyes while Claire Danes shot herself in the head.

"So tragic," she'd mutter. "So beautiful."

A black cloud of bitterness stormed through Tristan's mind and without meaning to, he snatched the play from Miss Warren's hands.

Her usually kind eyes narrowed in question, so he mumbled an apology and slumped back in his seat.

"I take it you don't like Shakespeare, Mr. Parker." She fought a grin.

"He's okay, I guess," Tristan muttered.

"Then what seems to be the problem?" Her head tipped to the side, her elegant fingers wrapping around the rest of the books she had to give out.

His face was turning scarlet—he could feel it. Curious gazes flicked his way. Harley, the annoying girl from his PE class, gave him a sympathetic smile. He averted his gaze, keeping his eyes down while scratching his forehead in an attempt to hide his face. With a shrug, he shook his head. "There's no problem."

His English teacher wanted to say more; Tristan could

tell by the way she hesitated at his desk. He glanced up and noticed her lips twitch before she pursed them to the side and kept moving down the aisle, handing out books and receiving a steady stream of thank-yous.

Thumbing through the worn pages, Tristan gave in with a sigh and opened the cover, shuffling in his seat and leaning over the text.

"Before we get started, can someone please give me a brief overview of what this play's about?" Miss Warren perched her slender behind against the front edge of her desk. Her legs stretched out before her; the skin-colored pumps and fitted cream skirt she was wearing made them sleek and attractive.

Tristan looked away. He wasn't the only guy in the school to think the young English teacher was hot, but he was probably one of the only ones who didn't care either way. He wasn't interested.

"Tristan, how about you?"

His blue gaze was icy when he looked at her, but she just smiled at him, tipping her head so her fine, sandy locks fell onto her shoulder.

He pressed his lips together but soon had to give in with a sigh. The fact that she was ignoring the three raised hands in the class was proof she wasn't giving him an inch.

Clearing his throat, he mumbled, "It's about these two young people who meet at a party and fall instantly in love, but they're not supposed to be together because their families hate each other. They get together anyway, everything falls to crap, and they kill themselves."

A few snickers rippled through the classroom and Miss Warren stood, once again fighting a grin. "Okay, brief and to the point. I take it you have a low opinion of this play."

"It's all right, I guess." His shoulder hitched.

She held the book up in her hand, gazing around the room as she spoke. "You know, people say it's one of the most romantic stories of all time."

Tristan scoffed, his jaw working to the side. He couldn't make eye contact with the delusional English teacher when she glanced back at him.

"You don't believe in romance? Star-crossed lovers? A passion that could last beyond the grave?"

Tristan's lips pressed into a tight line. The flurry of truths he wanted to unleash clogged his throat. He didn't want to trample on her fantasies with his bitter reality.

If only she knew that love was a crock. It fooled the heart, broke the heart, and then shat all over it.

The only thing about William Shakespeare's play that actually made sense to Tristan was the death part at the end, because if Romeo and Juliet had somehow survived and gotten away with it, they would have had to face the reality of living with each other and finding out that stars don't shine forever and true love doesn't last.

3

Stone-Cold

Burlington was a smaller town than Albany. Tristan thought he'd hate moving from New York to Vermont, but after only two weeks, he was finding his way pretty easily and kind of liked the small lakeside town—not that he'd admit it to anyone.

Pedaling through the intersection, Tristan leaned into the corner and sped down North Street. The high school was less than two miles from his new home so it was an easy bike ride there and back. His father couldn't afford to buy him a car and Tristan didn't want him to anyway.

It had been a struggle to buy the house they'd found a month ago, and his father's wage was only just enough for them to get by. He'd managed to secure a job as a caretaker at the University of Vermont, but it was hardly a high-powered position. In fact, he was only working part-time hours until more work opened up, and he probably wouldn't have even gotten the current job if one of his old high school buddies hadn't put in a good word for him.

Leon Parker had been born and raised in Burlington and hadn't planned on moving back, but then his life fell apart and all he could think of was returning to his roots. Being a loyal son, Tristan followed his father a couple of hours north, and so began his new "meat in the middle of a sandwich" life.

Rounding the corner onto Booth Street, Tristan eased on the brakes and slowed to turn into his new driveway. The house was a two-story white box with wood paneling, a small front porch, and boxed windows looking out over Pomeroy Park.

It was a typical New England home, built close to the sidewalk with a big yard out back, surrounded by huge trees that turned gold and crimson in the fall. Tristan's house pretty much matched every other home along the block, except for the one next door.

The dark green house, surrounded by a high fence and towering trees, was a mystery to him. He'd been curious since the day they'd moved in, and caught himself spying whenever he stepped outside. There wasn't much to see, really. The skeletal trees guarded the house like belligerent Marines who seemed reluctant to let in the sunlight. Come the summer when the leaves had all grown back, Tristan wouldn't be able to see anything. The best view of the house was from the front, but even then, he had to go on tiptoes to see above the fence line. Tristan always slowed to walk past it whenever he was heading that way.

The house was a box, much like his, but there was an old-world, magical essence to it. Tristan figured it was most likely the sharply steeped roof or the intricate vines creeping up the exterior. Or it could have been the circular tower built into the east side. The dark green paneling and elongated Georgian cross-windows made it appear cartoonlike. Whoever built the house must have had creative passion and flair. A few years ago, Tristan would have hoped the house had some kind of mystical story surrounding it, but he knew better than to believe in fairytales.

Lifting the garage door, Tristan walked in and leaned his bike against the tool bench before pressing his palm against the hood of his father's car.

Stone-cold.

Tristan glanced at his watch and frowned. Sucking in a breath through his nose, he pulled the garage door closed again and jumped up the three steps before entering the house through the kitchen door.

"Hey, Dad," he called, slipping the bag off his shoulder and sliding off his gloves and jacket. The snow had pretty much gone for the year and spring was definitely on the way. Tristan was looking forward to warmer weather.

"Dad?"

Lightly kicking his bag out of the way, Tristan walked towards the low murmur of sports commentary coming from the TV in the living room. His father's long body was slumped on the couch, a can of beer in one hand and a remote in the other. Baseball season had just started up. Tristan stared at the screen with a bitter frown. A couple of years ago, he would have been flopping down on the couch next to his old man, settling in for the last three innings of the Yankees game.

But not anymore.

"I'm home." Tristan nudged his father's broad shoulder and forced a grin.

"Hey, buddy." His father squinted up at him. "How was school?" He looked back at the TV, slurping on his beer while Tristan tried to figure out if his father even cared what the answer was.

Ignoring the question, he bent down and picked up the two empty beer cans on the floor. Snatching the chip bag next to them, he scrunched it in his hand and walked to the trash can that was housed beneath the kitchen sink.

"Sorry about that, man," his father called over his shoulder. "I was going to clean up when I was done."

"Whatever," Tristan mumbled. "What time did you get home?" he called from the kitchen.

"What?"

"What time did you get home?" he snapped, using the need to raise his voice as an excuse to let off a little steam.

"Around two," his father yelled back.

Tristan looked at the pile of dirty dishes scattered across the kitchen counter. Half-eaten cereal was crusted to the side of the white bowls while coffee dregs stained the inside of the *World's Best Dad* mug. Tristan's upper lip curled. He hadn't had time to do the dishes before he left for school and now he'd have to fit that in along with cooking dinner.

With a heavy sigh, he leaned against the beige counter and gazed out the kitchen window, trying to decide exactly when the man he'd grown up idolizing had turned into such a loser. He'd always thought the downhill slide had started on the *day from hell*, the one Tristan was desperate to forget. But sometimes he couldn't help wondering if maybe it had started before then.

Scrubbing a hand over his face, he pushed off the counter and went to pour his father a large glass of water. He placed it on the coffee table, right by his father's feet, and hoped his silent message was loud enough. Tristan wasn't too keen on reliving the humiliation of having to call in sick for his hung-over father on the man's second day of work. That night his dad had apologized profusely and promised to never let Tristan down again, but as far as Tristan could tell, it was a pretty half-assed promise.

Tristan cleared his throat.

"Yeah, yeah, I'll drink it, okay?" His father scratched at his salt-and-pepper locks, his square face scrunching. "You don't have to worry about me. I'll be hauling my butt off to work in the morning...*on time*."

Tristan curbed his sigh, letting it ease through his lips

slowly before turning back for the kitchen. He had no idea what he was cooking for dinner, and it didn't help that it was the last thing he felt like doing.

"By the way, your mom called."

Tristan froze at his father's muttered words. He slowly turned while his dad reached for the glass of water and gulped it back. Shoving his hands into his back pockets, Tristan waited in tortured silence, unwilling to move back into the living room. Whatever conversation they were about to have, it needed to be over quickly.

"She said she's been texting you but you haven't replied?"

Tristan's gaze shot to the floor, his nostrils flaring as he prepared to argue his case.

"Look, man." His dad sighed. "I know you don't want anything to do with her right now, but..." A thick swallow cut off his voice.

Tristan glanced up in time to see his father's lips press together. His pale brown eyes were desperate. "She's coming to get you on Friday after school. You're spending the weekend in Albany."

"I've already told everybody I don't want to do that!" He looked away from his father's blurry gaze, willing him to turn back and keep watching the damn game.

"She's supposed to have you twice a month. That's what was agreed. I can't go against that just because you don't want to see her. Please, just quit being so stubborn. You need to give up on this damn protest. She's your mom. She loves you, and she wants to see you."

"It's not her," Tristan muttered. "I just don't get why I

should have to stay with *him* as well." The words were hard to get out.

"Because they live together now." His dad's voice was dark and metallic as he pushed himself off the couch, nearly tripping over the coffee table.

Tristan jumped forward to help but stopped when his father raised his hand, silently telling him to back off.

"It's not like I want you to go either, okay?" His dad's forehead wrinkled, heart-wrenching pain distorting his expression. "But your mother only has so much patience. If you don't get your butt down to Albany she'll have me back in court before I can blink. She'll accuse me of indoctrinating you against her and drag out the fight."

"I'm sixteen! I don't have to see her if I don't—"

"Do me a solid, Tristan!" his father boomed. "I don't have the money for more legal bullshit! So you have to go, all right? You just gotta go!"

Tristan's insides coiled. He hated how loud his father's voice was. Before the *day from hell*, he'd never really heard his dad shout before. It was a thunderous, ugly sound, usually directed at his mother. He wasn't afraid of his old man or anything, but in order to keep at least some semblance of peace, he muttered a soft "Fine. I'll go."

Working his jaw to the side, Tristan stepped away, letting his father lumber past and into the kitchen.

No matter how old Tristan grew, he always felt small beside his towering father. He'd taken after his small-boned mother, and although he had a broad chest and shoulders like his dad, he'd never have the powerful presence.

He cringed as his father swung open the refrigerator door and grabbed another beer can.

If only his mother knew. She'd be all over it, claiming Leon Parker was a useless father and incapable of looking after their only son. His dad was right; she'd use whatever means she could to get Tristan back to Albany, but the court had let him decide and he wasn't budging.

His father—drunk or sober—was a million times better than his cheating mother and her stick-up-the-ass boyfriend.

4

When Anger Flares

Tristan pressed his back against the wall and let his father barrel past. The big man flopped back onto the couch and resumed his baseball-watching, beer-slurping marathon. He spent most evenings doing exactly that, drowning his empty sorrow with beer and the distraction of TV.

Tristan hadn't known it would be quite like this when he chose to leave New York and move to Vermont. After the *day from hell*, when his parents first separated, he'd been given no choice but to live with his mother. His dad had found out about the affair and left the house, totally devastated. Tristan had then had to suffer a year of back and forth between his parents. Angry, toxic words, hours of accusations and name-calling. He'd heard it all. Walls and shut doors couldn't hide it from him.

When the divorce proceedings had finally started, Tristan hadn't expected to even have a choice. When the lawyer first offered it to him, he was almost paralyzed by what to do. His mother had been on one side of the shiny, black table, her wide, blue eyes pleading with him while his father had sat on the other looking lost and desolate.

It'd been the hardest decision he'd ever made, but it was the only one he could. His mother had a boyfriend. It didn't matter that they'd gotten together when she was still married; they'd remained a couple, happy and in love while his father was ripped apart at the seams. Besides, she had an inner strength and ambition...unlike his dad. If Tristan hadn't chosen him, his old man would have been left with no one—a poor, lonely wretch living on Fruit Loops and beer.

"I'll start dinner," Tristan mumbled, pushing up his sweater sleeves and shuffling into the kitchen.

There was no point fighting over his mother. It only made his dad drink more, and Tristan didn't want to have to lug him up the stairs later that night. Thankfully his father wasn't an angry drunk. If anything, liquor made him snore like a freight train...or cry like a girl who'd been dumped at the prom. Neither choice was appealing.

Checking the refrigerator, Tristan snatched the last

couple of beer cans and tucked them under his sweater before grabbing his father's car keys off the hook and sliding them into his back pocket.

"I just forgot something in the garage," he called. "Back in a sec."

Sneaking out the kitchen door, he trotted down the steps and went around the back of the garage, emptying the last two cans and squishing the metal down for recycling. He was pretty sure he could convince his dad they'd run out of beer. He'd managed to do it before. The car keys were safely in his back pocket too. His father wouldn't look for long before giving up and mumbling something about buying more beer the next day.

His father had always been quick to quit on a cause, which was why he probably walked out on his wife, even though *she* was the one who'd cheated and should have been booted out the door.

Throwing the flattened cans into the recycling bin, Tristan stopped to look across at the mysterious house. If he rose to his tiptoes he could see the edge of the tower poking out above the winter trees. He wondered what was up there. Probably just an old attic filled with broken furniture and dust-covered boxes. Once-priceless treasures that had been discarded for something newer and shinier.

Anger fired inside of Tristan's chest as he pictured his mother and her new boyfriend locking lips like high school sweethearts.

"Stupid assface," Tristan muttered, turning back for the house.

He was nearly at the stairs when he caught a

movement from the corner of his eye. Whipping around, he spotted the baseball just as it landed in the driveway and rolled to his feet.

Emotions clogged his throat as he slowly reached down to grab it. Running his thumb over the red stitching, he pushed the ball into his palm. It felt so familiar. How many thousands of times had he caught and thrown a baseball in his life? The hours he used to play catch outside with his dad. The endless practices and games his parents ran him to. It had been his number one priority. He'd been obsessed...until everything fell apart.

Because of lies and deception.

Because his mother and her boss were so wrapped up in their own pleasure that they didn't stop to think about how it would affect anybody else.

Tristan's nostrils flared. He gripped the ball and hurled it with a loud shout. He didn't even think about where he was aiming. He certainly didn't expect the little white ball to sail across to the mysterious green house and fly through the open attic window.

He cringed and hunched his shoulders, relieved at the lack of shattering glass. He felt like an idiot for losing his temper. With all the shouting and angry outbursts he'd been dodging over the past year, he'd learned to internalize everything, to shove his emotions down deep so they couldn't rise to the surface and hurt anybody.

"Hey!" A young, disgruntled voice caught his attention.

Tristan's eyes flicked towards the mailbox. A young boy, who looked about ten, glared at him. "Was that my ball?"

"Uh..." Tristan swallowed and walked for the back steps.

"Hey! No fair! I want my ball back!" Pounding feet on the pavement stopped him from going inside.

As easy as it'd be to escape into the house, he didn't want some precocious kid pounding on the door and disturbing his dad. Tristan couldn't guarantee what his father might say or do. He didn't want to face the embarrassment when his father did something to trigger a wave of street gossip.

He rolled his eyes and spun around as the kid puffed to stop behind him. The boy's face was round like a basketball, his skin tinged red by anger, the cold wind, or overexertion. It was probably a combination of all three.

Tristan flashed him an apologetic smile and shrugged. "It's just a ball, kid. I'll give you one of my old ones."

"I don't want one of *yours*. That was my ball. You had no right to throw it away. I want it back!"

"Then go ask for it." Tristan pointed at the house.

The kid's brown eyes rounded like dinner plates as he slowly looked over his shoulder. "Are you crazy?"

"What?" Tristan frowned.

"Hey, Matty! What's taking so long?" a small kid with freckles and a shock of red hair yelled from the other side of the street.

"This dick threw my ball at *that* house!" He pointed his chubby finger behind him while Tristan frowned.

He was about to tell the kid to watch his mouth when the little redhead gasped and ran over to them. "No way.

Not that house."

Tristan took in the boy's pale expression, his face wrinkling with confusion. "What's so bad about that house?"

"You don't know?" The chubby kid shook his head like Tristan was an idiot.

He gave him a sharp glare before gazing at the dark, green residence with its army of trees and wraparound vines.

"It's haunted," Little Red whispered.

5

The Haunted House

Tristan snickered. "There's no such thing as ghosts."

"Yes there are!" Little Red argued. "There's a ghost in the attic. It's a young girl who was murdered and she hasn't left earth yet 'cause she wants to see her killer avenged." His green eyes bulged.

Tristan bit his lips together, struggling not to laugh at him. Clearing his throat, he shook his head with a skeptical smirk.

"It's true! Danny Birkman told me."

"I believe it." The chubby kid scratched the side of his

neck, looking twitchy. "Sometimes you see a pale-faced girl with white hair floating around in the tower."

"What?" It was impossible for Tristan not to be cynical. They were talking like it was reality and not some ghostly legend that'd been passed down over the years.

"The curtains are always closed in that place and you hardly ever see anyone come in or out. I mean, sometimes stuff gets delivered there, but no one ever leaves."

"I was peeking through the fence once and I saw a lady come out onto the porch to collect a delivery. She looked real mean."

Tristan gave the boys a droll look. "If the house is really haunted, why would she stay there?"

"Because the ghost is her daughter," Little Red whispered, his voice a spooky warning.

The boy next to him shivered, rubbing the mitt up his arm and chewing his lip.

"Okay." Tristan rolled his eyes, scuffing his Converse on the rough concrete, ready to head back inside and get on with dinner prep.

"A man used to live there too, you know, but no one's seen him in years." The chubby kid's nose twitched and he shot a nervous glance over his shoulder. "What's the bet she killed them? And buried the bodies in the basement."

"Or locked them in a trunk in the attic!" Little Red was so convinced. He scratched his freckly nose and then started biting his thumbnail. "Maybe we should just forget it. It's just a ball."

Tristan was about to agree and once again offer one of

his old ones to replace it. He was pretty sure he had a box of them buried in the bottom of his closet.

He pointed his thumb towards the house and was about to speak when the ball's owner started to protest.

"What? No!" The boy's face scrunched. "My grandpa gave me that ball. I can't lose it!"

Little Red crossed his arms. "Well, I'm not going in there."

"He threw it." The kid pointed at Tristan. "He should go get it."

"Agreed."

They both nodded and Tristan was tempted to tell them to stick it. But the little kid with his chubby cheeks and wide glassy eyes looked like he was about to cry or something.

Guilt nibbled, an incessant feeling that he knew would only get worse if he didn't do something about it.

"Dammit," Tristan muttered between clenched teeth.

The little boy sniffed and started blinking. Tears were a fast-approaching threat. Tristan didn't want any trouble. If he didn't go and get that damn ball, the two kids would run home to tell on him. Geez, that was the last thing he needed, some pissed-off father pounding on his door, demanding to know why he'd thrown his son's baseball away.

"Okay, whatever. Just... I'll go." Tristan pushed between the boys and jogged down his driveway.

"Be careful!"

Tristan shook his head with a light snigger and then paused when he opened the gate. He gazed up at the tower. Thick vines wrapped around the exterior, making it look pretty climbable. But the polite thing to do was to knock on the front door.

It was ridiculous to feel scared or creeped out by the kids' insane stories, but as the tall wooden gate squeaked shut behind Tristan, he couldn't shake the disquiet that had taken up residence on his shoulders. The loud click of the gate lock closing made him flinch. He walked up the concrete path, overrun with unkempt grass and weeds, and then climbed the front steps. A shiver skittered down his spine as the top step creaked beneath his weight.

The porch needed a fresh coat of paint. The brown varnish beneath his sneakers was so thin and worn he could see the boards of wood. In fact, the entire house looked as though it needed a spruce up. Thick cobwebs laced each corner of the overhang, dead leaves and the odd bug dangling from the white silk.

Tristan's Adam's apple felt swollen in his throat as he swallowed and rapped his knuckles on the thick door. It was stupid, but he had his fingers crossed that no one was home. Although the stories were just that—stories—being so close to the house made Tristan's nerves sizzle.

He gazed at the large brass doorknob stuck into the center of the wood. The brass was engraved with a leafy pattern that looked old-world, although it suited the quirky house perfectly.

He could picture gnarled fingers wrapping around the knob on the other side—bony white knuckles and razor-sharp nails.

"Don't be an idiot," he muttered, pulling his shoulders back when he heard the thump of feet on the hardwood floors.

A series of clicks followed, and then the door lurched open about two inches. It was being held in place by a chain and only gave Tristan a narrow view of the woman's sharp face. Her clear blue eyes scrutinized him with a glare that made him swallow and take a step backwards.

"Hello." He forced a smile that probably came out looking like a grimace.

"What do you want?" Her accent was posh, like British royalty or something. Her tone was icy, but she had a soft voice. It was a weird combination and totally unnerving.

Tristan cleared his throat. "Sorry to disturb you, ma'am. I was just wondering if you could check your tower...attic thingy for a baseball. We think it went in your window."

Her fine eyebrows pulled together in a tight frown. "You broke one of my windows?"

"No, ma'am. It was open. The ball just kind of flew straight through."

"It was open? On a freezing-cold day like this?" Her eyes rounded, fear skittering across her expression. "Excuse me, I must go."

"But the ball?"

"No! Find something else to play with. You shouldn't be hitting balls towards the houses anyway."

Tristan raised his arm with a sheepish smile. "It was an accident. Please, can I just—"

"No!" she snapped again. "I must go."

"But—"

The door slammed shut. Tristan sighed, scratching the back of his head with a confused frown. Pursing his lips, he wondered if he should try again, but he was pretty sure she wouldn't bother answering him a second time.

He spun on his heel, shoving his hands into his worn jean pockets and jogging down the stairs. He opened the gate and walked straight into the two anxious boys.

"Whoa!" Little Red fell onto his backside.

His friend bent down to help him up while Tristan closed the gate.

"Sorry, guys. I don't think we're going to have much luck."

"Oh no, Matty." Little Red looked at his friend, his face bunching with sympathy as the bigger boy started to cry.

"Dad's gonna kill me."

"It's okay, man." Tristan shrugged. "I'm sure he'll understand. Hey, I'll even replace it with a brand-new ball. How about that?" He lightly tapped the boy's shoulder, trying to coax a smile out of him—anything to ease the guilt knotting his stomach.

"You don't get it! That was Grandpa's last gift to me. I wasn't supposed to be playing with it outside, but I really wanted to hit a home run with it. He would have loved that." Matty sucked in a shaky breath, slashing tears off his dirty cheeks.

Tristan frowned, feeling even worse. His guilt was only amplified when Little Red muttered, "His grandpa died a couple weeks ago."

You've got to be kidding me.

Tristan clenched his jaw and looked over his shoulder at the house. He narrowed his gaze at the vine-wrapped tower and wondered.

Don't be an idiot.

Matty sucked in a shaky breath as a fresh wave of tears lined his lashes and began to fall.

Shit! Be an idiot, then!

Clearing his throat, Tristan ignored the voice in his head and gave the boys a tight smile. "Don't worry about it, kid. I'll get your ball back."

"How?" His lips quivered.

"Those vines are pretty thick. I think I can climb up to the window."

"Are you crazy?" Little Red squeaked. "What about the ghost?"

Tristan chuckled and headed for his driveway, calling over his shoulder as he went. "Just stay here, all right?"

Running past his house, he wove around to the back of the garage. He couldn't just waltz straight onto the property. The posh lady was no doubt watching from her window.

His best point of entry was over the back fence, as far from the house as possible.

Jumping up, he grabbed the edge of the tall fence and scrambled up the wood. He vaulted over the other side and landed in the unkempt lawn. The long grass swallowed his Converses as he snuck towards the house.

The Ghost in the Tower

Dry sticks and dead debris snapped and crackled beneath Tristan's feet while the ominous trees loomed large. Dusk was just starting to set in, the blue sky a shade darker than it had been an hour earlier. It gave the disheveled yard a creepy vibe and Tristan questioned himself several times as he snuck towards the vine-wrapped tower.

Why the hell was he doing this for some kid he didn't even know?

He moved forward anyway, staying low and eyeing the

house for any sudden movements. It was probably intrigue more than anything that had him stopping at the bottom of the tower and analyzing the vines. They were a thick mass of interweaving roots. Tristan ran his fingers over the rough exterior, skeptical it could hold his weight. Then he noticed a rickety trellis buried beneath it all. It probably couldn't hold his weight either, but maybe the combination of the vines and trellis together would be enough.

Gazing up the tall tower, Tristan couldn't deny the sense of danger and the voice of reason screaming at him to back away. He ignored it, placing his hands against the trellis and pulling himself up until he could reach a decent enough foothold. Shoving the toe of his shoe into the tiny trellis cavity, he leaned into the vine and used the power in his legs to push a little higher.

He'd always been a good climber—long and lean, with strong muscles that weren't bulky. It was easy for him to bear his weight. His mother had spent years calling him a monkey and laughing nervously before ordering him to not climb so high.

His lips twitched at the memory and he pushed himself a little higher. Yeah, it was risky—the vines could snap or rip away from the house at any moment—but he struggled to think when he'd last felt so alive.

He was climbing up a forbidden tower that quite possibly housed a ghost. That was kind of cool.

With a grunt, Tristan pulled himself up the last few feet, until his fingertips were gripping the dirty window ledge. Shuffling up the rest of the vine, he tiptoed on the top rung of the trellis and hauled himself through the open window.

Gripping the edge of a low bookcase, he wriggled his legs and pulled himself through, landing with a thud on the shiny wooden floor.

His face bunched with confusion as he studied the immaculate attic. Overstuffed bookcases lined the walls, but they weren't covered in dust. A trunk sat in the corner, clothes neatly hanging on a freestanding rack behind it. A large desk with a computer was sitting in the corner next to a high shelf that housed labeled trays— English, Math, Humanities...

Tristan looked behind him, his lips parting at a luminous living space that housed a comfy-looking sofa and a huge pile of pillows.

Every surface was spotless, not a speck of dust or grime to be seen.

What kind of attic is this?

Tristan rose to his feet, wiping his grimy hands on his butt and easing into the room. He had to be quick, grab the baseball and run, but curiosity pulled him farther into the room. Peeking his head around the corner, he spotted a craft table laden with beads, buttons, ribbons, wonky scissors, stamps, and every colored card imaginable. Hanging above it on clear, nylon strings were a collection of perfectly constructed origami cranes. Tristan tipped his head, enchanted by the way they spun and swayed. Stepping towards them, he lifted his finger to touch one. That's when he spotted something out of the corner of his eye.

It was just a shadow in the edge of the room—at least he thought it was, until it moved.

He jumped back with a gasp, his heart thundering in his chest as he caught sight of a large pair of pale green eyes.

He backed away from the ghostly white hand reaching for him and crashed into a wooden chest, losing his balance and tumbling onto his backside.

"Stay back!" He scrambled away from the ghoulish creature, his breath evaporating as it stepped into the light.

It was the girl.

The one who was murdered by her mother.

Ghosts do not exist! This is insane! I don't believe in ghosts!

Tristan's mind screamed the words while his pounding heart and light head told him he was lying.

The ghost's long blonde hair, so pale it was nearly white, hung over her skinny shoulders, reaching down to her hips. She was wearing a navy blue turtleneck sweater, making her white skin look even more translucent. Her skinny legs were wrapped in pale pink tights and she was wearing a pair of fluffy UGG boots.

It was a weird thing for a ghost to wear, but maybe she'd had them on the day she died. The guys failed to tell Tristan she was a teenager. At least she looked like one anyway. Kind of pretty too.

She took a step towards him, her green eyes lighting with a soft smile.

"S-stay back." Tristan raised his hand to stop her.

Her lips rose into a playful grin, her pointy little nose

twitching when she laughed. "Shouldn't I be saying that to you? You're the one who just broke into *my* house." She had an accent, much like her mother's, but not quite so strong and la-di-da.

The ghost is talking. Oh crap, the ghost is talking to me!

Tristan's vision was blurring as a dizzy fear swamped him.

"Please don't kill me." He swallowed. "I just came to get a baseball. I swear, I won't come back again."

"Kill you?" Her thin eyebrows wrinkled. "I'm not that annoyed."

"I know what you are." Tristan pointed at her, his finger trembling.

"You mean a girl?"

"A ghost," he whispered.

She giggled, a sweet, melodic sound. "I'm not a ghost."

"Don't trick me." Tristan's blurry vision made way for a spark of anger. The room came clear as his survival instincts kicked in.

"I'm not." She spread her hands wide. "Here, look." Stepping past him, the girl moved to the couch and collected something from between the cushions, holding it out with a triumphant grin.

Tristan studied the baseball in her hand, but was distracted by her radiant smile. It took over her entire face, raising her cheekbones, narrowing her eyes and emitting such a sunny vibe that it was impossible for his lips not to twitch in return.

"If I was a ghost I wouldn't be able to hold this, would I?" She giggled.

Still trying to wrap his brain around the bizarre experience, Tristan rubbed his eyes and fumbled to his feet.

She stretched out her long, pale fingers. "Go on, touch my hand. You'll see I'm real."

He shook his head. It had become his instinctual response to most things of late, so it kind of happened before he realized.

"Chicken." Her smile grew even more dazzling as she laughed a little harder.

Tristan couldn't stop staring at her, entranced by the way her pale green eyes danced as she teased him.

As the unexpected fright wore off and made way for his standard skepticism, Tristan started to think logically again. It was a huge relief, and Tristan had to fight a smile as the crazies fluttered out of his head. Reaching forward, he took her hand, the pads of his fingers sliding over her soft palm before he wrapped them around her slender hand.

She gripped back, her smile softening. "I'm Helena Thompson."

"Tristan Parker," he croaked.

"Well, my crazy new friend, it's nice to meet you." She winked, and something inside of Tristan started to unfurl.

7

A Shining Light

"Helena," Tristan repeated her name softly.

She nodded. "It means shining light, which I think is simply beautiful, so I do my very best to live up to that."

Tristan's lips twitched with a bemused grin.

"Do you have any idea what Tristan means?" Her face was so open and innocent—wide green eyes, elegant eyebrows the palest brown. There was something very enchanting and beautiful about her.

It was hard not to stare.

She tipped her head, looking like a curious sparrow as

she studied him.

Tristan blinked and forced his eyes to the wooden floor. Finally he registered her question and shook his head. "No, I don't."

"Oh. Well, I'll have to look that up later, but in the meantime let's just make something up." Her eyebrows rose and she looked to the ceiling in thought, oblivious to the fact that she was still holding his hand and acting like no other teenage girl he had ever met in his life. "How about faint-hearted wanderer?"

He grimaced, his head jolting back. "What? No. I don't—that's awful. I don't want to be that."

"Hmmm." She tapped her chin. "You're right, not very complimentary, but so far that's all I know of you. However, I'm sure you can change my mind." Her grin captured him again and he was rendered speechless.

"Let's see." She let go of his hand, replacing it with the baseball before walking to the window. Tristan slid the ball into his hoodie pocket and rubbed his thumb and forefinger together as he watched her glide across the room.

Placing her delicate hands on the frame, she peered out the window, her hair forming a curtain around her. Tristan was still completely mystified by the strange girl, but it was a pleasant mix of intrigue and wonder.

She popped back into the room, flicking her hair out of her face and pulling it over one shoulder.

"Well, I must say, the climb was very impressive, so for that I am going to change the meaning of your name to faint-hearted adventurer." She grinned.

He frowned. "I'm still not loving the faint-hearted part."

Her expression turned from gleeful to astute, her eyes taking on a compassionate glow. "Me neither, but we're going to work on that."

Tristan's lips parted, his brow creasing with confusion.

A creak on the stairs below made Helena flinch. Her green eyes bulged for a moment before she caught herself and flashed Tristan a jumpy smile.

"Now who's faint-hearted?" His eyes narrowed, his expression smug.

Helena rolled her eyes with a self-deprecating smile. "There's a difference between being fearful of a *non*-ghost and knowing you're about to face a dragon."

"A dragon?" Tristan glanced over his shoulder at the attic door.

"Just go," she whispered, gripping his arm and genuinely looking scared.

He hesitated, suddenly swamped by an overwhelming urge to move in front of the beautiful girl. He needed to prove her faint-hearted theory wrong.

"Please." Her fingers dug into his upper arm as she tried to yank him towards the window. "Go."

He nearly tripped over her, catching her fragile body against his chest and steadying them both. Her expression melted to a look of wonder, her long fingers stroking his arm as she gazed at him. A loud creak just outside the door broke the spell and snapped her into action.

She jumped out of his arms and pushed him towards the open window before shuffling across the floor.

Tristan swung his leg out, sitting on the sill, reluctant to leave.

She flicked her hand at him, her expression cresting with panic as the door handle turned. She snapped away from him, her fine hair rising in the air as she spun.

With a silent curse, Tristan shuffled out the window.

"Is everything all right?" Helena's question was high and pitchy.

Tristan cringed as he carefully slid down the edge of the tower, clinging to the window ledge as he struggled to find his footing.

"For God's sake, Helena, I was up here only moments ago closing this window! It's too cold, and you know I like everything shut up by nightfall."

The wooden frame snapped shut just as Tristan's fingers left the sill. Clinging to the vine, he leaned against the house and sucked in a relieved breath. The faint sound of muffled shouting made him cringe.

He hated the idea of anyone yelling at that sweet girl, and couldn't imagine why anyone would want to raise her voice at such a fascinating, captivating human being.

Captivating? What am I, a poet? What the hell is wrong with me?

With a rueful grin, Tristan shook his head and began a careful descent. As soon as he was confident he could jump and land without snapping anything, Tristan let go of the trellis and dropped to the ground, bending his knees to soften the blow.

Sneaking back the way he came, Tristan looked over his shoulder one last time, hoping for a brief glimpse of

Helena. But the tower window was empty, and all he could hope was "the dragon" hadn't done anything to harm her.

As he climbed the fence, Tristan was haunted by the flash of fear in her eyes. He landed on the other side with a pensive frown.

"Hey! He's back! He's back!"

Tristan didn't even make it halfway down his driveway. The two boys bounded up to him, talking at the same time and throwing questions at him like he was the President at a news conference.

He dug into his pocket and held up the baseball in an attempt to shut them up.

It worked.

Sort of.

They went silent for a split second before letting out two breathy "whoas." Tristan handed the ball to Matty, who smiled at him like he was his new hero.

The kid was too amazed to speak, staring at the precious ball and then back up at him while blinking furiously to ward off the tears.

"Don't worry about it, kid." Tristan buried his hands in his hoodie pockets.

"Did you see the ghost? You were gone so long we thought she might have eaten you." Little Red's thin lips parted as he waited for the juicy story.

Tristan scoffed and shook his head, gazing over at the "haunted" house.

The truth was on the tip of his tongue, but for some reason he wasn't ready to share it.

Instead, he shrugged. "No ghost, guys, just an old attic filled with junk. That's why I took so long—the baseball had rolled under a couch and it took me a minute to find it."

"Wow. You're so brave." Matty finally found his voice.

"Yeah." Tristan's reply was a half-hearted whisper.

Not according to the blonde princess in the tower he wasn't. He wished he could figure out how to prove her wrong. He wished he could figure out why he even wanted to.

With their game restored, and no hope of a decent ghost story, the boys raced back to the park. Tristan let them go, waving when they turned to shout a final thank you.

Trudging up his back steps, Tristan placed his hand on the kitchen doorknob and looked over the fence to the tower that housed a shining light. His stomach bunched into a tight knot—a mixture of curiosity and wonderment. He wasn't sure if he wanted to see the strange girl again. Being called faint-hearted was hardly something to return for, but as he stepped into his house and lost sight of the tower, he couldn't shake the feeling that something was going to pull him back there again.

Fainted-hearted

Tristan parked his bicycle outside school and bolted it to the stand. Hitching his bag onto his shoulder, he prepped himself for another day. He wasn't really in the mood for school, but when was he ever?

To his bewilderment, all he felt like doing was jumping the fence and climbing a tower. It was all he'd been able to think about the night before as he lay in bed listening to his dad snoring on the couch downstairs. He hadn't had the strength or willpower to move the big guy, so he'd covered him with a blanket instead.

He'd even dreamed about Helena—her pale green eyes that sparkled when she smiled, and the way her wisps of blonde hair had clung to her cheek before she brushed them behind her ear. Her regal voice haunted him as he slept—the whisper of a princess promising to turn him into a brave knight.

Tristan's eyebrows dipped and he shook the idea from his mind.

Brave knight, he scoffed. One chance meeting and it was turning him into a thespian playwright!

Taking the concrete steps two at time, he shuffled past a gaggle of high-pitched, squealing girls, wrinkling his nose and cringing. He'd never understood how chicks could get so excited about seeing each other in the morning...and how much they had to say to each other after less than twenty-four hours apart.

Veering left to avoid a football rocketing across the quad, Tristan scuttled around the bench seats and headed through the front entrance. As the gray day was left outside, he squinted against the bright florescent lights and the chaotic noise of the school corridor. The morning rush was always the worst. He coped by keeping his head down and trying not to bump anyone as he wove through traffic.

His shiny blue locker was in the third corridor on his left. He swiveled his hips and turned sideways to squeeze past a couple of seniors who were having their morning make-out session before taking a left and slowing his pace.

He looked up, prepping himself for what would no doubt be an attack of the Mikayla friendlies. Instead what he saw made his eyebrows dip into a sharp glare.

"Please, just give it back." Mikayla reached up, looking midget-sized next to Owen Stalwart. The guy was probably around the same height as Tristan, but he was broad across the chest and fat around the belly. Plus he had this cheesy white smile that bordered on maniacal. The weird thing was, he only ever showed it around Mikayla. Tristan still didn't know all the school gossip and he honestly didn't care, but after two weeks, he had figure out that Owen liked to torment the pint-sized junior and no one ever stepped in to do anything about it.

"Owen, come on, please?" She jumped up, trying to grab her precious binder from his hand.

"What, you mean this?" He flicked it over his shoulder, laughing like a hyena while Mikayla's shoulders slumped. The binder landed with a thud, loose papers spilling free and flying around the corridor. She dropped to her knees and started gathering the crumpled worksheets and scribbled notes.

Owen bent down, gently tucking her shoulder-length hair behind her ear and whispering something. Mikayla's cheeks burned red and she flinched away from him, her face bunching into a tight scowl.

Tristan's fingers tingled as he fought the urge to form a fist. He didn't want to get into any kind of fight, even if he could take out the arrogant senior. He hadn't come to Burlington to stir up trouble. So he hung back, even looking away when Owen stood and caught his eye.

Owen turned and sauntered down the hallway, calling over his shoulder, "Think about it, sweetness."

Mikayla shuddered, wiping her chin on her shoulder and glaring at Owen's back before reaching for the last of her scattered paperwork with shaking hands.

Tristan stepped forward, crouching down to retrieve the final few pages. He kind of felt like he should ask if she was okay, but he didn't want her to start crying. Girls did that when you checked on them, took it as permission to open up and start venting. The second the tears appeared, you had to stay and hear them out, even if you couldn't do anything to help them.

Clearing his throat, Tristan silently handed the papers over, feeling like a jerk for not saying anything.

"Thanks," she mumbled.

Her wide brown eyes were moist, but she sniffed and blinked a couple of times, shoving the papers haphazardly into her binder—so unlike her.

Brushing the hair off her face, she did another shudder as if remembering the guy's words.

She caught Tristan's gaze on her and shrugged.

"Ex-boyfriend stuff," she murmured, stepping to her locker and burying her face inside of it.

"You dated that guy?" Tristan couldn't help asking. It was impossible to hide his surprise.

"Don't ask me why I did it." Her voice sounded small and hollow, growing in volume as she slammed her locker closed and faced him. "All I know is that I'm going to regret it for the rest of my life."

"Or at least until he graduates." Tristan gave her a half-hearted smile.

She mirrored it, shaking her head and walking away

without even offering to show him to his first class.

He would have rejected the offer, even if she had asked, but the fact that she didn't made him feel like crap. A heavy lump formed in his stomach. Swinging open his locker, he rearranged his books, checking his schedule and pulling out what he needed.

Faint-hearted adventurer.

He shook his head. If Helena had been standing by watching that exchange, her name for him would have probably changed to cowardly wimp. He cringed, slamming his locker shut before shuffling off to class.

Who cared what the girl thought anyway?

Shoving his hands into his pockets, he couldn't deny that...he did.

9

For the Sake of Peace

The rest of the week went by without any drama. As much as Tristan wanted to climb the tower again, he resisted the urge. He didn't want to admit his lack of action over the whole Mikayla/Owen debacle and score himself an even more shameful name.

Shouldering the kitchen door open, Tristan dropped his bag on the floor, in its usual spot, and walked through to the living room. He was kind of relieved his dad wasn't home. His mother was due to collect him in a half hour and he hated the idea of them encountering each other for even a nanosecond.

As much as he was dreading the weekend, he wasn't prepared to put his dad under any more financial pressure. He'd bailed on two weekends with his mom already and wouldn't get away with a third.

"Just shut the hell up and get it over with," Tristan muttered as he hurried up the stairs. He snatched a duffel bag out from under his bed and shoved a few clothes into it. The idea of spending the entire weekend with her and her boyfriend made his skin crawl, but if he didn't go...the war would only get worse.

He balled up a sweater and shoved it into his bag before zipping it closed with an angry snort. Running a hand through his short dark locks, he scanned the room to make sure he had everything before bolting down the stairs. He hitched up his loose jeans and pushed up his sweater sleeves as he barreled into the kitchen, yanking open the refrigerator and checking on the drinks situation.

Only four beers—good.

Plus, there was enough spaghetti bolognese leftover to feed his father dinner. He could get takeout on Saturday, and Tristan would be home in time to organize something on Sunday.

Lifting the milk carton, he shook it and winced, annoyed with himself for not buying more on the way home. He snatched a pencil out of the glass next to the telephone and scribbled a note to his dad.

Hey.

With Mom for the weekend. Dinner in fridge—cover with a paper towel and heat for 2 mins in the microwave. You need to buy more milk and grab some eggs too.

See you on Sunday...if I survive.

T

Feeling like the parent, he smacked the note—at his father's eye level—onto the fridge, then spun when he heard the sound of a car engine. It was all about the quick turnaround. He wanted to be on the road and driving for Albany before his father even pulled onto Booth Street.

Grabbing his school bag, he threw it over his shoulder and carried his duffel bag in the other hand. His mother was just getting out of the car as he jumped down the back steps.

"Hey, Mom." He gave her a tight smile.

"My darling boy." She grinned, clipping over to him in her shiny black heels and taking his face in her hands. He gritted his teeth when she kissed his cheek and squirmed out of her hold when she took his shoulders to study him. "You're looking skinnier."

He rolled his eyes. "I'm fine. Let's go."

He stepped out of her grasp, walking around to the back seat and throwing his stuff inside.

"Do you need a jacket or something? Are you warm enough?"

"Mom, come on. Let's go." He yanked open the car door and slumped into the front passenger seat.

Her dark blue eyes narrowed and she shook her head

as she no doubt lamented the fact that he was in the "surly teenager" phase.

"Is your father home?" She slipped into the car, staring up at the house...probably trying to find fault with it.

"No. He works late on Fridays."

She threw Tristan a skeptical look. "Working or at a bar somewhere?"

Tristan sighed, his lower jaw jutting out. "He comes home."

To drink.

But Tristan wasn't about to say that.

"I just want to make sure he's taking care of you." She brushed her manicured fingers over his sweater sleeve.

"He is, Mom. You don't have to worry. Can we just get going, please?"

"Okay, fine." She sighed, starting up the engine of her swanky new BMW. She'd done pretty well out of the sale of their old family home. She'd been able to move in with her boyfriend, so half the house had simply turned into cash for her. Dad, on the other hand, had chosen to buy a home in Burlington and stretch them to the max financially.

Tristan tried not to judge either side, although from the dark way he felt sitting in his mother's car, it was obvious where his loyalties lay.

"So, how's school?" His mother's voice was way too chipper for a Friday afternoon. Tristan could tell it was forced. He didn't used to see that in her, but after she'd been caught cheating, Tristan saw a whole new side to the woman. She knew how to put on a show. It was probably what made her such a good events manager. Her clients trusted her because she knew how to hide any kind of disaster from them. Thankfully she was pretty good at averting all disasters too...except when it came to her marriage.

Tristan crossed his arms and shrugged. "School's school."

"Have you made any friends? Are you happy with your teachers?"

"Yes and yes." Keeping the lie going with short, easy answers was the best way to bring the conversation to a close.

His mother braked at the end of the street, flashing him a dissatisfied glare before turning right and heading for the main road out of Burlington.

It was a two-and-a-half-hour trip south—a long, painful trip if Tristan didn't do something to fix it. Having an intelligent conversation and making up some bullshit about how happy he was weren't going to make the journey any better. It'd only make his mother jealous, and she would then try that much harder to get him to move back to Albany. But admitting the truth that he was mothering his father and dragging them both through each day would have them back in court before Tristan could blink. No, the best way to solve the problem was to keep his mouth shut...and put his headphones in.

Digging into his school bag, he pulled out his phone, shoved his earbuds in and cranked up his music. It pissed his mother off. He could tell by her white-knuckled grip on the wheel and the way her red-painted lips smashed together, like she was holding it all in.

She would. She'd keep her feelings locked up, because that's what she did with Tristan. Their relationship had become all about plastic smiles and a desperate need to woo him back to the mother side of the fence. He wasn't doing it. She had someone to keep her company at the end of each day and he'd be damned if his father was forced to come home to an empty house every night because she'd forgotten the meaning of the word 'loyalty.'

Turning up the volume a notch louder, Tristan kept his gaze out the window, watching the world rush by as he silently bemoaned the weekend he was going to have to fake his way through.

"Shannon, honey, where's the saffron?" Curtis, decked out in a chef's apron, was fumbling through the spice rack, trying to prove himself a cook as he prepared some fancy-sounding meal that Tristan was sure he wouldn't like.

Having spent an evening and another full day in the company of his mother and CEO boyfriend, Tristan was well and truly done. He'd mumbled his way through multiple conversations—mostly small talk about school and sports.

Once again, he'd had to justify his reasons for not trying out for the school baseball team. His mother couldn't swallow the fact that he wanted to focus on his studies, plus the fact that the season had already started and he'd missed tryouts.

"Go talk to the coach. I'm sure he'll understand."

"Mom, you know I was off my game. That's why I pulled out last season," he'd groaned.

"But don't you miss it? Baseball was your everything."

"Well, things change." He'd shrugged, slinking out of the room to avoid continuing the conversation.

Against his will, he'd gotten to know Curtis a little better. The guy had pretty much stayed out of the picture when the separation first happened, sneaking around after dark to see Mom when he thought Tristan was tucked up for the night. As soon as the divorce went through, he invited Shannon to move in with him—yet another reason why Tristan chose his dad.

It wasn't that Curtis was a nasty guy. He was actually nice enough and pretty damn intelligent. But he'd had an affair with a married woman and Tristan didn't care that they'd stayed together and were obviously in love. Curtis McNeal broke up a happy home, and for that Tristan felt obliged to eternally hate him.

"Can you put that thing down and set the table, please?" Shannon snapped at Tristan as she breezed past him into the kitchen.

He gave her a slow stare, finishing his game of Candy Crush before rising from the couch and stalking into the kitchen. His mother was leaning against Curtis and smiling, holding up a glass jar with dark orange tendrils in it. He gave her a sheepish grin and pecked her nose, which then turned into a lip kiss with a little tongue on the side.

Tristan grimaced, slamming the cutlery drawer hard in an attempt to break them up. It worked and they jumped apart, Curtis letting out an abashed chuckle before quickly stealing one last kiss.

His mother doused Tristan with a simmering glare. He turned his back on it and set the table in silence. Curtis started to hum, no doubt wanting to break the tension, but if anything it was grating on Tristan's nerves. He didn't know how much more of Mr. Happy he could take.

"Done!" He slapped his hands on the back of the chair, then spun for the couch. He slumped onto the pillows and had every intention of continuing his Candy Crush saga, but his mother ruined it by snatching the phone out of his hands.

"Hey." He lurched forward, trying to steal it back.

"I'm putting this away for the rest of the weekend. I can't handle your silence anymore. You've barely made eye contact this entire visit. I haven't seen you in nearly two months, even though you're *supposed* to visit us every second weekend! I'm not wasting this time competing with your phone!"

"Give it back, please." Tristan kept his voice as even as he could manage. He wasn't used to his mother getting pissy with him. She usually spent all her time trying to charm him, but he'd obviously crossed a line.

"We have something very important we want to discuss with you over dinner. Curtis has cooked us an amazing meal, and we are going to enjoy it together *as a family*."

"He's not my family," Tristan mumbled, tipping his head towards the chef.

"Well, he's mine, and you *will* respect him."

Like you respected Dad?

The words were sitting in his mouth but he swallowed them down, not wanting the battle. He'd heard enough yelling in his life and he wasn't interested in an all-out scream-fest. He knew how pitchy his mother could get. Her voice took on this feral, repulsive timbre when she really got going. He hated it.

Digging his toe into the plush carpet, he reached out his hand. "Give me back my phone and I won't use it at dinner."

Mom gripped it. "I don't want you using it for the rest of the weekend."

"What else am I supposed to do?" He made a face.

"Talk to us! Spend time with me! Or go see your old friends. Does Natasha know you're in town?"

"We broke up over a year ago, Mom." Tristan lurched off the couch and gently snatched the phone back with a look that told her she was deranged. As if he wanted to spend time with his ex-girlfriend, or any of his old friends. Did she not get it? Her betrayal had destroyed him. He'd had to live with the gossip surrounding her shame. He'd had to live with the rumors that his father had turned into a raging alcoholic because his slutty mother had screwed her boss.

He'd had to live with all that shit, and his only coping

mechanism had been to pull back and bury himself in solitude.

But of course he couldn't say any of that, so he sealed his lips and stared at the floor.

"Please, Tristan, just talk to me. I need to know how you're really doing. You're my son. I want to share my life with you."

He cleared his throat, his lips pursing to the side. Finally he lifted his phone and muttered, "I'll go put this away in my room."

She went to roll her eyes but stopped herself, crossing her arms with a sad smile. "But you're not going to talk to me, are you?"

"I'm sixteen. I'm not supposed to talk about my feelings." He tried to smile with his joke but couldn't really pull it off.

His mother's face crested with a slight show of agony before flashing with anger. "You're just like your father."

Tristan forced himself not to react, instead muttering, "I'll take that as a compliment," before brushing past her. "And don't worry about dinner. I'm not hungry anyway."

10

A Brewing Storm

Less than fifteen minutes later, his mom rapped on the guest room door. The sharp staccato sound was loud enough to puncture the music blaring in Tristan's ears. With a soft curse, he rose from the bed and shuffled to the door.

Flinging it back, he glared at his mother, grimacing when he spotted Curtis behind her, his hands resting on her shoulders. "What! What is so important that I need to eat a meal with you guys to discuss it?"

Curtis forced a calm smile. Tristan could tell by the

way his right eye twitched that it was an effort. "Son—"

"I'm not your son," he spat, gripping the door handle so tightly the metal ridge dug into his palm.

"It's just an expression, Tristan," his mother snapped. "Would you just shut your mouth and listen, please?" Her biting tone disappeared, nervous energy pulsing from her as she looked up at Curtis and gave him a tender smile.

Curtis met her gaze, his expression so loved-up it made Tristan want to gag. He squeezed her shoulder. "I've asked your mother to marry me." His eyes remained on Shannon while Tristan's stomach plummeted down to his shoes. He clenched his fist, fighting the dizzy spell trying to drop him to the floor.

That would kill his father.

Curtis looked across to him, his gooey smile making Tristan sick. "We wanted to tell you before we told anyone else."

Tristan swallowed, sour words clogging his windpipe. His gaze danced from the guy who'd come in like a leech and torn their family apart to the two-faced woman he was struggling to call 'mother.'

"Well?" His mother smiled, her eyes dancing with expectant hope. "Aren't you going to say anything?"

All Tristan could do was swallow and slam the door closed. He shut out their deluded happiness, even going as far as locking the door to prevent them from trying to win him over. The buds were back in his ears as soon as he reached the bed and he cranked the volume so high he was sure his eardrums would be damaged by the morning, but he didn't care. Anything to drown out the nightmare unfolding even further.

Irritating was the best way to describe Tristan's drive home from Albany on Sunday afternoon. After the rude way he'd treated his mother and her boyfriend over the weekend, she should have been bawling him out and not inviting him back, but in her usual fashion she decided the best form of discipline was to try and woo him with extravagant offers and gifts.

"Curtis and I were thinking of buying you a car."

"Why?" Tristan tore his gaze away from the scenery outside.

"So you can get around more easily." Her chipper voice was strained tight, the plastic veneer already cracking.

"I don't even have my license yet," he muttered, slumping further into his seat.

"Why not?" Her voice pitched high.

He shrugged, his jacket rustling. "Haven't gotten around to it."

"Well, get around to it."

"I like my bike."

"You can't bike to Albany." Her manicured fingers slashed through the air. "This is a long way for me to come every two weeks, and it'd be great if you could drive yourself down."

It was logical reasoning and Tristan really should have said yes, but he was still in a belligerent mood after his plastic-coated weekend.

"I don't want Curtis buying me a car," he finally muttered, his gaze traveling back to the window.

"What is your problem with Curtis? He's been nothing but nice to you!"

Tristan clenched his jaw and stayed silent.

His mother huffed and tapped her nails on the steering wheel.

"The car would be from both of us, not just him."

Tristan still didn't budge, his blue eyes trained on the tractor rumbling through a field in the distance.

"You can't punish me for wanting to move on with my life," his mother snapped.

He gripped his knee, his fingers digging into the denim as he fought the urge to explode. He kept his gaze out the window and eventually his mother gave in with a loud tut and a huff.

The irritating vibes buzzing through the car were replaced with an icy silence for the rest of the trip. Thankfully they reached the borders of Burlington soon enough. Tristan sat up in his seat, eager to get the hell out of the BMW.

With another disgusted tut, his mother pulled into the driveway and cut the engine, snatching at Tristan's jacket sleeve before he could escape.

"Look, I'm sorry if the engagement has come as a shock to you, but Curtis makes me really happy and it would mean the world to me if you could please get on board with this."

Slowly turning to her, he studied her desperate expression, locking away his feelings. His head jerked with what could have been deciphered as a nod, but the movement was minimal enough to be questionable. After a thick swallow, he muttered, "Mom, it's your life. You can do what you want with it."

Her head tipped with a cynical frown. "That's what your mouth is saying, but your eyes tell me something different. Are you ever going to forgive me?"

His jaw worked to the side, his tongue feeling thick and pasty. Clearing his throat, he shouldered the door open and mumbled, "Thanks for the weekend."

"Wait, let me walk you in." His mother scrambled to undo her seatbelt.

He paused by the back door of the car, a sudden anxiety whistling through him. "Why?"

"So I can see how you're doing. I want to see your room." She smiled, flicking her door closed.

Tristan's eyes narrowed to tiny slits, his mouth pulling into a tight line. She didn't care about his room. She wanted to check up on Dad. He yanked the car door open and snatched out his bags, shuffling towards the house on reluctant feet. His mind scrambled for ways to get rid of her.

"Mom, you don't need to come in. My room is boring, just a desk and a bed."

"Really? What about all your baseball posters?" Her hand rested on the thick wooden railing as he brushed past her and up the front steps.

He dropped his bags on the front porch with a sigh. "You don't care about the posters, Mom. You just want to check on Dad."

Her cheeks grew red, her lips spreading with a strained smile as she looked to the ground and fiddled with the chunky car key in her hand. "All right, fine." She glanced at him, clipping up the steps. "I want to make sure he's looking after my son."

Tristan tried to block her way, subtly shifting into her path. "He is."

Her blues eyes narrowed, her right eyebrow arching high—never a good sign. Her painted nail tapped him lightly on the chest. "You know, when you say it like that, it makes me think you're lying. What are you hiding?"

"Nothing." Tristan frowned. "I just don't want you guys to fight."

"Oh come on, we're over that now." She breezed past him, opening the door and waltzing in the front entrance like she owned the place.

Tristan grabbed his bags and hustled in after her, a little freaked out by what she might find. His head popped up behind her shoulder and he cringed.

His father was on the couch, his socked feet on the coffee table, his big toe exposed through the fraying fabric. Three beer cans were lined up next to his feet, one fallen over and empty while another was resting on the arm of the couch, his long fingers wrapped around it. A baseball game was blaring out of the TV so loud he didn't even hear them come in.

"Hey, Dad," Tristan called.

"Oh hey, buddy!" Dad raised his hand and started talking before he turned to face them. "Come check this out, the Yankees are killing these gu—" His eyes hit Shannon and he lurched off the sofa, tugging at his shirt in a feeble attempt to make himself presentable. "Shay." The edge of his mouth rose with a gentle smile, his gaze softening at the corners as he whispered her nickname.

Tristan's heart splintered and it was an effort not to let the emotion show. Clearing his throat, he pointed at his father's dirty shirt behind his mother's back. It took his dad a second to work out what he was silently saying, but he finally glanced down and let out a bashful chuckle, brushing the chip crumbs onto the floor.

Tristan's mother crossed her arms, a marked frown on her narrow, pointed face.

Scratching the short locks on the side of his head, Leon looked at his ex-wife—fleeting hope dancing in his eyes. "So, what—what are you doing here?"

"Dropping Tristan off, of course." His mother's hard tone dashed any promise of reconciliation. If only his father knew the whole truth. Tristan silently begged his mother not to say anything about the engagement.

His father sensed the hostile vibes and his defenses went up, surrounding him in quick formation like they always did. His chin bunched, his gaze turning stormy. "I mean what are you doing in my house?"

Shannon rolled her eyes, doing nothing to help the situation. "Oh please, Leon. I'm just making sure it's clean."

He stood a little taller, pushing out his broad chest

while his nostrils flared. "We're doing okay. You don't have to worry."

"How many empty beer cans are on the coffee table right now?" She pointed past his father's scrappy jean-clad legs to the littered table at his knees.

"Mom, leave it, please." Tristan's whisper was ignored as she stepped farther into the room, noting another two cans at the foot of the sofa.

"Geez, Leon! Are you drunk?" Her hands flew into the air before slapping onto her hips.

"Of course I'm not drunk. I've had a few beers while watching the game! Everybody does that." His father's hands started waving in the air as well. A storm was brewing and Tristan couldn't do a thing to stop it.

"If you are intoxicated I am taking this back to court." Shannon's pointer finger looked like a wand, aimed straight at her ex-husband's heart. "I will not have my son in your house if you can't look after him!"

"It was his choice to come with me!" his father barked. "The court said he could decide. You take this back there, it's just going to cost us a shitload of money we don't have!"

"Watch your mouth! And I don't care what it costs. This is about the well-being of *my* child, who seems to have turned into a surly mute since moving in with you! And why hasn't he started up baseball again? His talent is being completely wasted!" Her pointer finger landed on Tristan. He flinched away from it, slowly backing out of the room.

"That is his choice." His father's deep voice grew a

notch louder, sounding like thunder in the small living space. "I'm not going to force him into something he doesn't want to do anymore."

"He's sixteen; he doesn't even know what he wants. He needs guidance and if you loved him—"

"If you think I care about him any less than you, you're delusional. He's my son too, Shannon! I'm not the one who started screwing my boss, okay? You're the reason he quit. You broke up this home, not me!"

"Do you think I would've been interested in anybody else if you'd paid *any* attention to me? A little conversation goes a long way, Leon!"

It shouldn't have surprised Tristan that the old arguments reared their ugly heads within ten minutes of his parents being in the same room.

With a resigned sigh, he slipped away from the maelstrom, making a beeline for the back door and escape. He didn't know where he wanted to go; he just didn't want to be near them.

Closing the kitchen door behind him, he dropped onto the concrete steps and sucked in a few lungfuls of chilly air. His breath puffed out of his mouth like white smoke. He followed the disappearing wisps and found his gaze on the dark green tower next door.

Images of Helena's dancing smile played in his mind and before thought could stop him, he lurched from his spot and traipsed towards the fence, climbing the wood and jumping into the unkempt backyard.

11

Tell Me Your Sorrows

The climb was easier the second time around. He remembered his footholds and managed to make it up the tower without too much effort. The only problem he encountered was at the top when he found the window firmly shut.

He tapped on the glass, hoping Helena was inside. His fingers started to ache as he hung onto the sill and he was ten seconds away from giving up when a smiling, pale face appeared behind the glass.

Her grin was magnificent, making Tristan feel

instantly better. Sliding the window up, Helena reached out and helped Tristan inside. He tried to come through gracefully but ended up catching his foot on the sill and thumping onto the floor.

Helena giggled, the delightful sound chasing away his humiliation.

"Welcome back." She bent over him, offering her hand. Tristan gazed at her milky white fingers and shot her a quick smile before gently wrapping his icy digits around hers.

She didn't say anything, giving his hand a little squeeze before pulling him over to the sofa. She plopped onto the plush cushions and tugged him down beside her. It wasn't until he was nestled down and facing her that she let go of his hand.

Tristan hadn't expected to feel any kind of loss, but it was an effort not to reach out and take her warm fingers back into his. He sufficed by stretching his arm across the back of the sofa and picking at a loose thread poking out of the seam.

Helena tucked her legs up beneath her, bouncing a little as she got herself comfortable. Her playful smile coaxed Tristan's lips into a grin.

"I was hoping to see you again. I've been looking out for you."

"I've been away this weekend." Tristan stared out the window over Helena's shoulder and mumbled, "At my mom's place."

He scratched at his hairline, pushing the ribbed beanie farther up his head. He didn't want to look at

Helena. He feared his troubled gaze might somehow mar her pure beauty. She didn't need to be tainted by the crap he was going through.

"Tristan, I'm so sorry." Her delicate fingers caressed his arm, her thumb rubbing slow circles over his jacket.

Confused by her response, Tristan ran the words he'd just said over in his head but couldn't find any cause for her reaction.

"What are you—? Sorry for what?"

She shifted her head, catching his eye and magically holding his gaze. He blinked, trying to break the spell, but each time his lids popped open his gaze tracked straight back to her compassionate smile.

"Your parents are divorced, aren't they? I can see how much it hurts you, and I'm sorry you have to live with it."

Unnerved by her intuition and the weird power she seemed to have over him, he settled for a nonchalant head wobble. "I'm okay. It doesn't—I'm good."

"No, not really." She chuckled and then winked at him. "But you will be one day. As long as you don't let it eat you alive."

Her posh accent made him grin. He wanted to reach up and brush his fingers down her porcelain cheek.

What? Where was that coming from?

He let go of the thread and curled his fingers into a ball, digging his nails into the palm of his hand.

"So, where are you from?" He lifted his chin at her. "Your accent's pretty strong."

Her green eyes sparkled and she brushed a wisp of hair off her forehead. "My mother is from Cambridge in

England."

"How long have you been living in America?"

"About ten years." She grinned. "You're probably wondering why I don't talk more like you...but I like the sound of my voice. It's very regal, don't you think?"

Tristan's face bunched with a nonplussed expression that made Helena giggle. He couldn't help grinning. She wore joy with more beauty than anyone he'd ever known.

"Your two front teeth have a very small gap between them." She leaned towards his face, trying to eye his teeth more closely.

He clamped his lips together and scratched his upper lip.

"Oh don't be like that. I like it." She dipped her head, her skin blooming with a velvety redness. "Sorry, I really must learn to hold my tongue. I have a terrible habit of blurting out whatever's on my mind."

"It's okay." Tristan shrugged, wiping his mouth again and giving her a closed-mouth smile.

She grinned. The light filtering in from the window behind her made the edges of her hair glow with an ethereal quality that he couldn't help studying. He ran his gaze over her shimmering outline before coming to rest back on her perfect face.

"You really are very handsome, you know?" She studied him with open scrutiny. "With your dark hair and chiseled face. And those eyes, like a restless ocean."

Tristan looked down at his jeans, unnerved by her soulful whispering.

She tapped her long fingers on his knee, her short,

unpolished nails scratching the denim.

"Come, my new friend, tell me your sorrows."

Tristan glanced up at her. "Why do you talk like that?"

"Talk like what?" Her pale eyebrows rose.

"I don't know, in that weird, old-fashioned way."

Her eyes sparkled. Curling her fingers around her ear, she gave Tristan a shy smile and pointed at the overstuffed bookcase to his left. "I read a lot of fairytales and I like the way they talk. There's a magical musicality to the words that makes me smile. And why shouldn't I try to fill my life with things that make me happy?" Her grin grew with confidence, turning into a colorful bloom that reminded Tristan of tulips in the spring.

"I've never met anyone like you before." His whispered words were tinged with a wonderment he couldn't hide.

She giggled, her slender shoulders hitching. "That is a beautiful compliment and I shall treasure it."

"I was kind of saying you were weird." He snickered, embarrassed at the way he simply blurted the truth. He pressed his lips together and looked at the coffee table, trying to read the title on the spine in an attempt to hide his faux pas.

She forgave him with a pat to the knee, her eyes twinkling as she bent forward and grabbed his gaze with that magnetic power of hers. "Weird is unique, and unique is good. I don't want to be like anybody else."

He didn't know how to respond and ended up looking like a fool as he gave her a quizzical frown.

Her smile morphed to that compassionate one from

before and she reached forward, rubbing her thumb over the crease lines on his forehead. The pads of her fingers were soft on his skin, lighting small, tingling flames every place they touched. He froze on the couch, studying every inch of her exquisite face as she gazed at him.

"You know your eyes turn a little gray when you're sad. I wonder what color they are when you smile."

His lips twitched, rising into a lopsided grin as a short breath puffed out his nose.

"No, I mean a real smile. An unabashed, reckless, spontaneous smile that you have no control over."

His mouth dipped, his expression crumpling with an unspoken apology. He couldn't remember the last time he'd smiled that way. His lips had probably forgotten how.

"Poor Tristan." Her fingers brushed his face one last time before she sat back and tipped her head to study him. "Your sadness is a heavy burden. You must share it with me."

Tristan squirmed on the couch, tugging at his pant legs and trying to get comfortable. "Why would I want to do that?"

"Because a burden shared is a burden halved."

"You don't want to know my *sorrows*." His eyes rounded with the word and he rolled them. "I wouldn't want to put that on anybody."

"Oh, but I do." She leaned towards him, her eyes wide and earnest. "If I didn't, I wouldn't have asked you."

"You seem ridiculously honest for a teenager." He clenched his fist again, resisting the urge to reach forward and touch her.

She giggled, her eyebrows bobbing up. "Sometimes I don't know if it's a strength or a weakness. All I do know is that bottling things up can destroy your soul." Her merry expression faltered for a second, her face washing with a flash of sadness as she glanced at the attic door.

Tristan peeked over his shoulder, wondering what lay behind the dark wood and caused the ominous creaking on the stairs.

The dragon.

His stomach clenched and he was about to turn back and ask her about it when she stopped him by rising from the couch and moving to her desk.

"I, for one, believe very strongly in letting things out—both good and bad." Her fingers kissed the bottom of one of her dangling cranes. It swayed beneath her touch and she smiled lovingly at the origami bird before reaching for the one behind it.

"These are my victories, those moments in time you want to treasure for the rest of your life." She held the wing of the one closest to her, her lips twitching with a smile as she read something on the wing. "This was when I first learned to ride my bike and the sound of my father cheering me on." She moved to the one beside it, tipping the wing so she could read the inscription. "And this is the first time I read *The Princess Bride* and I fell in love with Wesley. I treated the book like a teddy bear until I'd read it at least ten more times." Helena giggled. "Oh, and this is the time I baked chocolate chip cookies from scratch with no help at all from anybody. A very proud moment indeed." She tipped her nose in the air, putting on false airs until a giggle gave her away.

Tristan rose from the lumpy sofa, stepping around it to take a closer look.

"Treasures," she murmured beside him, her face cresting with sadness before she pulled in a deep breath and pointed to the one dangling just past Tristan's shoulder. "That one's new."

Tristan turned to look at it. "What's it celebrating?"

"The time a strange boy climbed in my window and thought I was a ghost." She grinned.

Tristan's cheeks caught fire. He dipped his head, rubbing his face and letting out a bashful sigh.

She laughed, nudging him in the side with her elbow. "I'm sorry, I couldn't resist." She wrapped her arms around her tiny waist and swayed for a moment, her expression peaceful and content as she gazed at the paper cranes. "I hang them here to remind me of all the reasons I have to smile."

Moving to the window behind her, she leaned her head against the glass and pointed down. "Those are my burdens."

Tristan's face twitched with a frown. Sliding his hands into his pockets, he shuffled towards her, standing close so he could see what she was pointing at. Her soft breath tickled his neck, trying to distract him as he peered down at the slanted roof and clogged gutters. They were littered with white cranes. Some of them were still intact, but most were disintegrated by the weather, white clumps of rotting paper with bleeding black ink scratched onto the surface.

"Whenever something really tries to get the better of me, I write it on the wings and then throw it out the window."

Tristan glanced at her, his brow still wrinkled with bewilderment.

"I want to live with my victories, not my frustrations." Helena let out a short sigh and reached for Tristan's hand. They were still shoved in his pockets, so she sufficed with wrapping her fingers around his wrist. "I'm not saying throwing them out the window takes them away completely, but it is a good reminder that they can't own me. I may not be able to control everything in this world, but I can control what I choose to do with it. And I say burdens be gone." She looked over her shoulder, her gaze locking on the hanging birds above her desk. "And joys be treasured."

Letting him go, she moved to the old wooden desk and gathered a couple of cranes from the corner before spinning back and holding them out to him.

"Here, take them. Cover the wings with all the nastiness you had to endure this weekend and then throw them out the window. It'll be like watching your worries fly away."

Tristan kept his hands in his pockets. "I wish it was that easy."

"It is, if you'll let it be." She stepped towards him, her head tipping to the side as she bobbed her hand up and down.

He still couldn't reach forward to take them. He

couldn't quite make himself believe that writing it down and chucking it out the window would make anything better. He'd probably just end up feeling like a fool.

With an exasperated sigh, Helena stepped into his space and wrapped her hand around his wrist again. Her hair smelled like jasmine, turning his arms to compliant limbs of string. With an insistent tug, she pulled his hand out of his pocket. Laying the cranes in his palm, she gently wrapped his fingers around them.

Placing her fingers over his, she looked up at him, her bright gaze so sweet and sincere he couldn't tear his eyes away from it. "Trust me," she whispered. "I like you too much to fool you."

"You don't even know me," he croaked.

Her smile was soft as she reached for his face, her fingers gently resting on his cheek. "But I see you...and I like what I see."

The urge to lean forward and press his lips against hers was overpowering; he could almost taste the sensation on his tingling mouth—the soft, sweet pressure of her supple lips melting against his. He'd never been so intoxicated by a girl before.

"Tristan!" A sharp call from outside jolted him away from the thought. They both jerked, the spell between them shattered.

A creak on the stairs behind the wooden door made Helena's eyes bulge and storm with worry. "You should go."

She stepped away from him, her head bobbing, her eyes trained on the door.

Tristan reached out for her. "Wait, are you—?"

"Tristan! Where are you?" His mother's voice punctured the air below them.

"Go." Helena pointed at the window. "Your mother is calling."

"But—" He sighed, reluctant to leave her.

Catching his pained expression, she softened it with one of her smiles. "Please come back and see me again. I'm always here to listen."

"Why *are* you always here?"

The light in her eyes dimmed, the smile on her lips faltering.

"Tristan!" His mother's call was turning into an anxious bellow.

"Please, you must go." Helena pushed him towards the window, her touch firm yet kind. He stumbled towards the exit, not wanting to leave her, especially knowing he had to climb back down to reality.

"Are you going to be okay?" He stopped at the window, a sudden fear clutching him.

"Of course." She smiled. "As long as you promise to come back and see me again." She winked.

He nodded, finding the request a solemn one in spite of her playful wink. "I promise."

The words helped him turn away from her, the idea that he'd be coming back making it easier to climb onto the sill. Shoving the paper birds into his pocket, he shimmied out into the cold air. He took a moment to find his footing and began a careful descent.

"Write them down," she called to him. He looked up

in time to see her blonde locks tumbling over her shoulder. "I promise it will make you feel better."

She responded to his grin with a giggle before disappearing back inside. An unexplained warmth bloomed in Tristan's chest, that sense of wonder engulfing him as he climbed down the tower and landed in a thick lawn that was in desperate need of a cut.

12

Paper Crane Magic

"TRISTAN!" His mother was going to lose her voice if she didn't stop shouting for him.

Darting across the grass, Tristan scrambled up the fence and landed behind their garage. His foot sank into the soft earth at the edge of the building and he ended up walking through a cobweb as he darted into his backyard. He slapped at his skin, then wiped the back of his hand over his mouth before sucking in a breath, pulling his shoulders back and trying to hide the warmth racing through him by dragging his feet toward the house.

He appeared on the driveway just as his mother spun around, muttering a flurry of curses. She was staring at her phone screen, her nails tapping on the glass.

"I'm here." He shoved his hands into his jacket pockets and ambled over to her.

"Oh." She touched her chest. "I was worried you'd taken off and I wouldn't have a chance to say goodbye." She clipped towards him, depositing her phone back into her purse. "What are you doing out here? It's freezing."

"The yelling arguments are quieter from outside."

His mumbled explanation made his mother flush. Her nostrils flared before she pulled her lips into a tight smile.

"Sorry about that," she muttered, smoothing down her eyebrow and lifting her chin. There seemed to be a tickle in her throat as she gazed at the side of the white house.

"Did you tell him?" Tristan kicked at the concrete, wondering what he'd be walking into after his mother drove off.

She ran her tongue over her top teeth and then pursed her lips. "Now wasn't the best time. Your father isn't ready to hear about my life." She stepped forward, holding him at arm's length and giving his shoulders a little squeeze. "But you're welcome to tell him if you'd like to."

"I'm good." Tristan's reply was swift and sharp, accompanied by a pointed glare that made his mother let go and step away from him.

She scratched her collarbone and fingered her expensive gold necklace, rubbing her thumb over the diamond pendant.

"Think about the car offer. It'd probably make life easier on all of us."

Tristan's shoulder hitched and he shook his head. "I don't want Dad to feel bad."

Her head jolted back, a tendon in her neck pinging when she sniffed. "Why should it make him feel bad? You're my son too, you know. I have a right to look after you." She hitched her purse higher onto her shoulder. "This would be so much easier if you'd just move back with me."

"Someone's got to look after Dad." Tristan winced and scratched his eyebrow, worried he'd said too much.

His mother's eyes narrowed, her right eyebrow arching. "He's a grown man. He's not your responsibility, Tristan. He should be able to take care of himself."

Looking to the ground, Tristan scuffed the toe of his sneaker on the uneven patch of concrete and shrugged. "I like it here."

"Really?"

"Yes, really." Tristan glanced over his mother's shoulder, watching a minivan amble past their house. Little Red appeared in the back window, waving frantically. Tristan snickered and looked to the ground.

His mother whipped around to see what he was smiling about. Her lips dipped with a frown as she watched the back end of the car disappear down the road.

"Who was that?"

"I don't know his name," Tristan mumbled.

His mother huffed, rubbing her forehead and looking

older for just a second. "Okay, Tristan. You like it here. That's great." She flashed him a tight smile.

"If it's easier, I can take a bus down next time."

"No, I want to come and get you. It's fine." She blinked rapidly as she stepped forward and pulled him into a hug. "I just miss you, that's all." She sucked in a breath, her fingers digging into his shoulder blades. "I love you so much."

Her broken whisper made Tristan feel bad, but he still couldn't make himself hug her back...or say anything. His throat was clogged, his voice box holding a silent protest.

She gave him a final squeeze before letting go and then turned for the car, slashing at an invisible tear and sliding on her sunglasses as soon as she sat down in the driver's seat. Tristan waited until she'd reversed onto the street, raising his hand in farewell before spinning on his heel and heading into the house.

His dad was on the couch, staring at the television, his expression blank.

"You need anything?" Tristan tapped his shoulder.

"All good." His father nodded, his words clipped. Tristan didn't miss the way his long fingers dug into the armrest, and figured it was best to just leave him to it. He understood the comfort of silence. Talking things through didn't always make them better.

He clomped up to his room, the bags he'd grabbed from behind the couch feeling heavier than usual. Stepping into his room, he closed the door with his butt, then dropped his duffel bag and backpack before moving to the window. He couldn't see the green tower from the angle he was at, just his own desolate backyard—a small square of lifeless grass that needed some warmth and color. It wouldn't happen. The Parker men could mow lawns, but neither of them were interested in gardening.

Tristan pressed his head against the glass and pulled the cranes from his pocket. They were a little bent and crushed. He pressed one between his thumb and forefinger, straightening it out. It came back into shape pretty easily and he stared at it for a long minute before walking to his desk and pulling a pen from the black container in the corner.

Sliding into his chair, he nibbled on the end of the plastic ballpoint, gazing at the white crane until his vision blurred.

Blinking a couple of times, he sat forward and pressed the paper crane into the wood, writing:

Mom's getting married while Dad's getting drunk.
Curtis cooks with saffron and wants to buy me a car.
I hate Curtis.
I blame Mom.
I want Dad to change.

The wing was soon covered with his scribble, scratchy black lines that marred the white perfection of the paper. Holding the bottom between his thumb and forefinger, he lifted it into the air and then let it fall back to his desk. It dropped quickly, nose-diving into the nicked wood. A half-hearted smile tugged at his lips. Jumping from his seat, he walked to the window, wrestling it open with a grunt. With his breath on hold, he dangled the bird out the window. Doubt picked at him, reminding him how stupid the idea was. Dropping the crane wouldn't take his problems away.

"But they can't own you," he muttered, flicking the bird out the window before he changed his mind.

The light breeze caught the bird, flying it sideways and whisking it in a circle before letting it fall. It landed in the gutter, perching on a pile of rotting leaves that had yet to be cleared. Leaning against the frame, Tristan crossed his arms and gazed down at the bird. A slow smile grew on his lips.

His problems were resting in a rotting pile of leaves, exactly where they belonged.

A chuckle burst out of him and he stepped inside, slamming the window shut on the cold breeze and turning his back on the discarded paper crane.

13

Paranoia

Monday brought with it the normal madness—the hectic rushing out the door to get to work and school on time, the bustle and unspoken frenzy of students in the corridor as they realized they probably should have done more homework over the weekend.

The second half of the school year was in full swing and end-of-year exams would soon be upon them. No one wanted to admit it, but the underlying stress was there nonetheless.

In spite of this, Tristan cruised through his day, a light

freshness giving him a slight bounce. Nothing too obvious, just an internal air that he wasn't even aware of. A smile toyed with his lips as he unlocked his bike at the end of the day, and it slowly grew wider as he pedaled home.

He didn't even bother putting his bag inside. As soon as the garage door shut, he climbed the fence and ran—knees high—through the grass, climbing Helena's tower in record time.

Clasping the window ledge, he pulled himself up and spotted Helena on the sofa. She was lying down, bathed in sunlight and fast asleep. Her left arm was dangling over the edge, her long fingers curled above the book lying on the floor. The hard cover was propped up like a tent and the pages beneath were bent from being dropped.

Tristan smiled at the serene image. He didn't want to wake her, but the idea of climbing back down and not seeing her was too deflating, so in a show of outright selfishness, he tapped on the glass.

It took a few taps to rouse her, but when she sat up and spotted him, her face lit with pleasure and she raced across the room in her fluffy UGG boots to let him in.

"You came back." She held his arm as he eased in the window, landing on his feet—much to his relief.

"I promised I would." He gazed down at her, loving the sparkle in her light emerald eyes.

"Did it work?" She tipped her head like a curious sparrow.

"What?"

"The crane. Did you throw one out the window?"

He nodded, a grin appearing without his say-so.

"You're smiling." She pointed at him. "It must have worked."

"What color are my eyes?" He leaned towards her.

"Still a touch gray. We'll keep working on the smile." She patted his arm and spun, gliding back to the couch like a princess.

Tristan shook his head with a soft snicker and followed her.

She crouched down and collected up her book before dropping onto the cushions and tucking her legs beneath her.

"What are you reading?" Tristan slid the bag off his shoulder and pointed at the book.

"*Grimm's Fairytales.*" She held up the tattered novel, then lovingly swiped her hand over the cover before hugging it to her chest. "I must admit, I'm a little obsessed. My father gave it to me for my fifth birthday and he used to read to me every night before going to bed."

"I guess he doesn't do that anymore, huh?" Tristan held the edge of the old sofa, gently lowering himself onto it.

A sad wistfulness touched her expression and she whispered, "No."

Her slender fingers ran up and down the spine, a barely there frown tugging at her lips.

Tristan reached out and tapped her elbow, wanting to distract her before that sadness took hold. He wasn't sure he could handle seeing Helena cry. Suns didn't cry, ever—

they shone.

"Which is your favorite tale?" he asked.

Her gaze flicked to his, her sadness swept away by a grin. "Hmmm, how do I decide? I love them all for different reasons." She looked to the ceiling, tapping her chin. "But if I had to pick just one, I'd say...um..."

"Rapunzel?" He grinned.

She dropped the book to her lap with a delighted gasp. "How did you know?"

"Well, you kind of live in a tower." He brushed the tip of his finger through her wispy, long tendrils. "And your hair is..." He wanted to say 'beautiful,' 'enchanting,' 'breathtaking,' but swallowed the words before he embarrassed himself.

Her melodic giggle made him grin. "I do spend a lot of time up here, but it's my haven. I love it." She looked around the room, her gaze lingering on her paper cranes. The soft light streaming in the window gave the room a magical quality, and the breeze whistling in made her cranes dance and sway.

"Do you sleep up here?"

Her cheeks tinged pink. "Not usually. My bedroom's below us." She pointed at the hardwood floors. "Right under our feet." She breathed in a happy sigh, hugging her book to her chest and gazing around the room again. "I just prefer it up here. I feel safe...at home...in this place."

Baffled yet again, Tristan couldn't help making a face. "So you're not being locked up here against your will? Held hostage by some dragon lady?"

Tipping her head back with a laugh, she touched her stomach and chuckled some more, but the sound had a hard, unconvincing edge to it.

Tristan scrutinized her expression when she looked at him again. Her smile was in its usual place, her green eyes still bright and clear, but...

"No, I'm not a hostage. She may seem like a dragon at times, but she's just my mother. My overprotective—" Helena bit her lips against whatever else she was going to say and ended on a whisper. "—mother."

The answer was hardly satisfactory and didn't explain the flash of fear that took over her expression every time there was a creak in the stairwell.

Tristan shuffled in his seat, tapping his finger against her elbow again.

"Seriously, what's your deal? Why are you up here? Why do you never come outside?"

Her expression shut down for a second, her face going blank. Tristan half-expected her to kick him out the window, but her lips opened and closed a few times...like she was trying to decide how much to say. She glanced at his face, then averted her eyes to the cranes, blinking rapidly and licking her lower lip. "My mother doesn't like me to go outside. It's not safe."

"Not safe?" Tristan's stomach twisted.

"Yes." She swallowed, her knuckles going white as she gripped the book to her chest. "The world is full of evil people who want to hurt each other. We must stay inside." Her pale gaze ran around the room, her lips pressing together as she nodded. "Mother says these walls protect us."

The air in Tristan's lungs went stale, taking his usual sarcasm a moment to kick in.

He blinked a couple of times, his forehead bunching tight.

Helena's mother is crazy. Just my luck. I'm compelled to hang out with the daughter of a paranoid psycho.

"But—" He tipped his head with a frown. "But she can't do that to you, can she? I mean, if you really wanted to leave, you could, right?"

Helena shook her head. "Why would I betray her that way? I can't break her heart. I fear to think how she'd react if I tried to walk out the front door."

"Wait. You walking out the front door would break her heart?" He made a face.

Helena's fingers curled a little tighter around her book, her slender shoulders growing tense. "I don't think you realize how afraid she is."

"But she's being... Don't you think it's kind of selfish?" Tristan's eyebrows formed a wonky line.

Her gaze snapped towards him, her bright eyes intense. "Selfish? Her wanting to protect me is selfish?"

Tristan shook his head, glancing away from Helena's terse confusion. He didn't want to get into a fight. Licking his lower lip, he cleared his throat and asked, "Why—why does she think the world is evil?"

Helena blinked, her lower lip trembling. She caught it with her teeth, scratching the side of her nose before finally looking at him. Her gaze faltered and she blinked a few times before looking to the ceiling. She shrugged, then swallowed and licked her lips. "My father was murdered. About—about nine years ago."

Tristan's twisted stomach began to quake. Murdered. That was heavy.

Too heavy.

He went to rise from the couch, not wanting to face the conversation. He had his own troubles. He was looking after his soul-destroyed father. He couldn't take this on as well.

Helena snatched his arm with a gentle smile. "You don't have to be afraid. I've made peace with it—mostly." She tipped her head with a wry chuckle. "But my mother...she hasn't."

He let her win, plopping back onto the couch with a worried frown.

"He was shot, trying to stop a thief in a convenience store." She shook her head, her eyes glazing over when she whispered, "He left the house one day in his paint-splattered jeans and brown slippers. He was only supposed to be gone fifteen minutes, but he never came home." She sniffed. "He was a true knight, always willing to defend the weak. He was King Kenneth and I was his Princess Helena." Her lips trembled into a smile, her bright eyes glassing with tears.

Tristan's eyebrows spasmed as he fought to control his growing frown.

King Kenneth? Princess Helena?

The girl was... Tristan didn't know what she was, but he had a sinking feeling he couldn't handle her weirdness.

"They never caught the man who killed him, and my mother...she's so lost." The tremor left Helena's voice, her tone deepening as she went on to explain, "They were soul mates, you see, destined to love only each other until the end of time. When he was ripped from our lives, she went into hiding and took me with her." Helena dropped the book to her lap, tracing the swirling gold letters of the title with her forefinger. "She stayed strong until he was buried, and then she shut down. Aunt Sylvie came over from England and tried to persuade her to come home, but Mother wouldn't have it. She wanted us to stay in King Kenneth's castle." Helena's lips twitched with a grin and she shook her head as a deep sadness crinkled her expression. "I didn't mind so much. Mother's family is very wealthy and I'm sure they would have tried to send me off to one of those stuffy boarding schools where imagination and storytelling are not revered the way they should be." Her eyes rounded as if the thought alone was a criminal offense.

If his brain hadn't been so busy trying to wrap his head around what she was telling him, he might have smiled.

But he was frozen, expressionless, on the couch, trying to figure out how the hell he was supposed to respond.

Helena didn't notice his internal struggle. She was too wrapped up in her story.

"I was relieved Mother fought for me. But..." She bit her lip. "After Aunt Sylvie left, things changed. It started with small panic attacks when I left for school or blanking out at the grocery store. She withdrew from the world, cutting off her family and spending her days watching old home movies and poring over the photo albums Papa had made for her. She began ordering online and then asked me if I'd like to try homeschooling. I was in utter despair so I agreed without question and we fell into this routine. I never thought it would become a permanent thing, but..." Helena shrugged, her head bobbing like a robot. "It's okay. I like my tower." Her smile was fleeting and weak. "It's a sanctuary where I can be myself."

"Don't you get lonely?"

She glanced at him then grinned. "I have you."

Tristan shook his head, an unexpected anxiety clawing at him. "No, I mean, you've got to see that this is unhealthy, right? You can't stay locked in this house forever."

"It's what she needs right now." Her calm voice and contented smile irritated him. She was basically being held hostage and she was totally cool with it!

"But you're only...only..." He waved his hand at her.

"Fifteen."

"Well, that's insane." He shot off the couch, tugging down his sweater and pacing away from her. "You've got the rest of your life ahead of you. She can't lock you away from the real world."

"It's what she needs to do right now, and you know, maybe she's right. The world is full of evil people. My father was murdered for trying to be helpful."

Tristan spun around, planting his hands on his hips and getting ready to argue.

Her slender fingers rose into the air, stopping him

before he could speak.

"She can control the environment here. She can keep me safe. Fear has taken ahold of her and she believes that leaving the house will get us killed or hurt. She's just...trying to give us as many heartbeats as possible."

"That's insane." Tristan looked to the floor with a huff, digging the toe of his shoe into a jagged hole in the floorboards. "What kind of life is that? That's—" He kicked his foot and scratched his forehead, a righteous anger that he didn't quite understand pulsing through him.

It wasn't fair!

A girl that kind and beautiful deserved everything, and she was being locked away for no good reason. He tore his gaze away from the floor, catching her eye and giving her a desperate look he hoped she'd comprehend.

Her lips parted and she gripped the back of the sofa. "I know it's hard to understand, Tristan, but—"

"She can't do this to you. You deserve a normal life."

The imprisoned girl shrugged, her eyes glassing over with a resigned smile. "She needs me to comply. She's not ready to handle the idea of leaving the house and letting me go." She pressed her lips together. "I just... I can't see her fall apart again. If being here with me is what holds her together, then this is where I must stay." Tucking a lock of hair behind her ear, she bent her head and sniffed. "I don't always like it, but I love her. She's my mother, and I won't cause her any distress by fighting." Running a hand down her hair, she pulled the locks over her shoulder and began playing with the ends. A peaceful smile fluttered over her lips. "We like to think that he's still here, sitting with us at mealtimes, looking over my shoulder when I read. It brings me comfort, and I don't need more than that to be happy."

Tristan's face was tight with confused frustration. "How can you talk like this? How can you say those words with a smile on your face? You're crazy."

Her eyes snapped up, the warm green tinged with ice. "We all do what we must to survive."

"Surviving's not living. You can't spend your life this way."

She raised her chin. "I've accepted it. If you can't respect my choices, then maybe you should leave."

"Fine." Pacing back to his bag, Tristan snatched it up and fought the burning in his throat. Anger coursed through him, bashing into a wave of sadness that was trying to envelop him. He'd only known the girl for a fleeting minute, but the idea of never seeing her again was crippling. He knew better though. He'd been around enough fighting in his lifetime and he wasn't about to engage in more.

In spite of that, his knees were ready to buckle as he hobbled to the window.

He couldn't look at her. One glimpse of her face and he'd spin around, lurch back to the couch, and try to understand her plight.

But what was the point of that?

What was the point of letting someone in who could never leave her house? He had enough problems in his life; he didn't need to add a bucketful of crazy.

Shuffling out the window, he kept his eyes down, not looking up when he was sure she was above him. He clutched the trellis, scrambling down as quickly as he could.

It was ridiculous. He barely knew the girl. He shouldn't be feeling like his world was about to fall apart.

A snap sounded beneath him, his muscles tensing up as he lost his footing.

Helena gasped while he slid down the tower. His fingers fought for him, snatching a thick strand of vine and clinging to it. Struggling to find a foothold, he swung to the side and shoved his toe into a small opening that held him long enough to let him descend to a safer section of the tower.

He heard a sigh of relief somewhere above him but couldn't look up to check.

He'd been protecting himself against heartache for the last two years; opening himself up to a girl he couldn't be with was the worst thing he could do. He should never have gone back.

Shoving the kitchen door open, he clambered through the house, not even checking the couch to see if his father was there.

Screw dinner. The guy could eat peanut butter sandwiches. Tristan wasn't hungry anyway. Thumping into his room, he slammed the door shut and threw his bag into the corner. It smacked against the wall and dropped with a thud. He pressed his hand into the desk and closed his eyes, dipping his head and fighting for air.

When his lids popped open he spotted the cranes. He

probably should have reached for a pen, but instead he snatched the paper birds into his palm and made a fist, squeezing them out of shape before dropping them into the trash.

14

A Hateful Life

School was total shit. It had been all week. Three days after Helena's deranged news bomb and Tristan was still struggling to wrap his head around it. He was battered by guilt at skipping out on her, anger at her insane way of thinking, and sorrow at the thought of not being with her. Life was impossible. It hated him. Any time something good came to light it was snatched out of his grasp.

It made him want to retreat into a foxhole. Somewhere dark where no one could find him, need him, hurt him and tug at his heart.

Throwing his shirt on, he shoved the rest of his sweaty PE gear into his bag and zipped it shut. Hustling past the row of half-naked guys, he kept his head down and ignored the comments floating around him.

"Did you see Dana working out with the cheer squad this afternoon? Damn, man, that girl is fine."

"Shut up, dude. She's got a boyfriend. Besides, Harley is way hotter than that girl."

Flinging the door back, Tristan twisted out of someone's way and set a fast pace for his locker. He didn't care about Dana or Harley with their preppy good looks and flirty smiles.

There was only one girl occupying his thoughts, and she was out of reach.

The idea was bitter acid in his brain.

He wanted so badly to go back to his old life, where baseball ruled and his team was everything. Heck, he'd even take his ex-girlfriend Natasha if it'd kill the ugly feeling in his chest.

But it wouldn't...because he couldn't turn back time.

He couldn't make his mother *not* cheat, and he couldn't make his father *not* be a loser. Just the way he couldn't rescue Helena from her warped green castle.

Shit, I wish I could.

Gripping his bag strap, he kept his head down and hustled to his locker. All he wanted to do was get the hell out of school and hide away in his room.

He reached his locker without any more drama, only to find Mikayla leaning against hers. He would have said hello if it hadn't been for her blotchy cheeks and red nose. He didn't want to know. He had enough angst to deal with and couldn't take on anyone else's.

Flipping his locker open, he snatched out the copy of *Romeo and Juliet*, irritated with Miss Warren for calling him out in front of the whole class. So he hadn't done his homework the night before; did that really deserve a public reprimand?

Yanking the textbook out of his bag, he winced when he noticed his algebra test float to the floor. He hadn't meant to fail it; he'd just forgotten to study. He'd had a lot on his mind over the weekend!

Snatching it off the floor, he balled it up and threw it into his locker before slamming it shut. Mikayla jumped, her small shoulders tensing.

Mumbling a barely audible apology, Tristan brushed past her and headed for his bicycle. All he needed was for the damn day to be over!

The bike ride home was quick and reckless. He nearly got taken out by a pickup truck and had to pull onto the curb and swerve around a pissed-off pedestrian to avoid getting squashed. He stood up on the pedals, cycling hard to get away from her bellowed insults.

Little Red, Matty, and a posse of kids were out playing ball by the time he zipped into his driveway. He ignored their invitation to join them, shouldering the back door open and hightailing it up the stairs.

Once again his bag got flung across the room. He threw his gym clothes into his laundry basket and cursed, hating the idea that he'd be the one to have to clean it all later, hating that his dad's laundry would be piled up near the washing machine as well.

"I'm not your mother!" he shouted at his closed door. Lashing out with his foot, he knocked the trash can over. Balled-up paper and a few gum wrappers tumbled onto the carpet along with two crumpled cranes.

His shoulders slumped, breaths spurting out of his nose as he knelt to the ground and collected them up like they were delicate petals.

"You can't sacrifice your life for her," he whispered. "If she's stuck in that tower, nothing could ever come of it. You'll never be able to take her out. You'll never be able to do anything with her!" He squeezed his eyes shut and smashed his teeth together. "But I hate the idea of never seeing her again."

Then why are you in your room and not climbing my tower right now?

Her posh accent made the words ring in his mind. Her eyes would sparkle as she said them, a slight exasperation tinging her tone.

Jumping to his feet, he gently laid the cranes down on his desk before yanking his door open, nearly tripping as he sped down the stairs. Not wanting to get spotted by the baseball boys, he snuck around the back of his garage and stayed low, climbing up the edge of the tower so as not to get spotted.

The window was a little ajar and he wrestled to shunt it open, hoping none of the kids would look up from what they were doing.

The sound of their shouts and laughter floated over

him as he struggled to squish through the little gap he'd created. A few grunts and a lot of upper-body exertion later, Tristan was lying on the attic floor.

Craning his neck, he looked around the room, hoping to spot the girl who'd captured him, but she was nowhere to be seen.

"Helena?" he called as loud as he dared.

Nothing.

He spun onto his stomach, pushing off the floor and jumping to his feet.

The attic door was half open. He crept towards it, straining to hear voices. He thought he heard the faint sound of laughter.

Laughter.

Joy...in spite of the crazy.

She was only doing what she thought was right. Hadn't he done the same by choosing his father? Pressing his forehead against the door, he closed his eyes and muttered a soft curse.

He'd been such a dick about the whole thing.

He wished he could go down and see her, apologize on the spot, but her mother would flip out. Helena had to know he'd come though.

Rushing to her desk, he shuffled some papers around until he found a writing pad. Tearing a fresh sheet from the back, he grabbed a pen and scribbled her a note.

Your decision scares me. I worry that you're throwing your life away.

I'm worried I won't get to see you again.

Sorry for being faint-hearted.
Help me find a new name, Helena. Please.

He scribbled down his email address, which consisted of his first name, middle initial, and last name. Very boring. Hers was probably *princesshelena* or *shiningstar*—if her mother even let her have an email address! He cringed, hoping she did. He hated the thought of leaving things unresolved for a second more than they had to be.

Folding the note in half, he wrote her name on it and slipped it inside the book on the coffee table. All he could hope was that the dragon lady didn't find it before her daughter did. He needed Helena to know he wasn't giving up on her. As petrified as he was of seeing her—connecting with her again—he was more scared of never looking into those green eyes or smelling that hint of jasmine in her hair.

15

My Heart Doth Swoon

Darkness had settled in for the night. Dinner had been served and the dishes rinsed. Tristan could vaguely hear the whir of the dishwasher as he sat up in his room and tried to read the next scene from *Romeo and Juliet*. The soft glow from his computer, plus the amber lamplight, illuminated his desk. He hunched over the tattered book, his thumb playing with the bent corner of the page he was on.

"*O, she doth teach the torches to burn bright,*" Tristan mumbled. "*It seems she hangs upon the cheek of night. Like a* rich jewel in an Ethiope's ear; Beauty too rich for use, for earth too dear!" Dropping the book with a sigh, he scrubbed his face. "What the hell does that even mean?"

Scanning the rest of Romeo's little paragraph, Tristan tried to decipher what he could but was distracted by a bleep from his laptop. Moving the cursor to his mailbox, he clicked on the icon and grinned.

His stomach twitched, a smile cresting over his lips.

PrincessHelena - he'd been right.

Pointing the cursor on Helena's email address, he double-clicked and leaned towards the screen.

What does the A stand for?
~ H

That was all the message said. No greeting, no farewell, aside from a letter. It was a very random start to what would no doubt be a very entertaining conversation. It took Tristan a moment to work out what she was asking and it wasn't until he spotted his email address that he realized what she meant. With a little snicker, he rested his fingers on the keyboard and typed:

Alex. Tristan Alex Parker.
~ T

He pressed Send and waited, tapping his finger over Romeo's lines.

An eternity passed—Tristan was sure of it—before his inbox dinged again.

You'll be pleased to know that Alex means defender of men...a fine name and one that will fit you well. But I have better news yet...Tristan means a knight! So, my faint-hearted adventurer, I am pleased to inform you that your name officially means a knight and defender of men. How absolutely perfect! The wheels were set in motion the day your parents named you. All you need to do now is start living up to such a magnificent title.
~ H

Tristan's eyes danced with wonder, his heart blooming in his chest as he replied.

You have a way with words that enchants me. I've never thought the meanings of names had any significance until I met you. You are a shining light and I haven't been able to stop thinking about you, because my world is dark when you're not near.
~ T

He cringed, the cursor hovering over the Send button as he reread his babble. Squeezing his eyes shut, he pressed the mouse and bit the inside of his cheek.

Well, well, I'm turning you into a poet. This is indeed a hanging crane moment.
~ H

He snickered, rubbing his hands together and leaning

over his keyboard.

I doubt you could ever make a poet out of me. I'm trying to read Romeo and Juliet right now and it's painful! Why couldn't Shakespeare just talk like a normal person? His writing is so hard to understand. I'm drowning in 'doths' and 'thous,' and random words tacked on to the end of sentences that don't make any sense!
~ T

Shakespeare was a genius! And Romeo and Juliet...my heart doth swoon!

I love that play! Yes, it is hard to decipher, but don't rush through it. There is beauty in those words. A beauty that has been lost throughout the years, replaced with words like 'forshizzle' and 'true dat.' Don't get me wrong, those words can still make me smile, but they've not been kissed by magic.
~ H

Sitting back in his chair with a bewildered smile, Tristan snorted a puff of air out his nose and shook his head.

She was seriously like no one he had ever met in his life. An old-fashioned fairytale, trapped in a world that would never understand her.

Skimming his fingers over the play, his eyes landed on Romeo's final two lines.

"*Did my heart love till now? Forswear it, sight,*" he murmured, "*For I ne'er saw true beauty till this night.*"

A smile grew on his lips, broad and unfamiliar.

Are you still there? I was hoping you could tell me about your week.
~ H

Tristan made a face, his lip curling as he bent over his keyboard and started tapping.

My week. You don't want to hear about my week. It's been awful.
~ T

Well, now I'm intrigued and you must share it with me— every miserable detail.
~ H

Sitting up a little straighter, Tristan gave a pensive frown, then poised his fingers over the keys and went to work, describing everything he could, but mostly focusing on his particularly heinous day. He tried to pepper it with sarcastic humor, but she read right through it.

It was a good thing you came to see me, then. I'm sorry I was not there to hug you and tell you that 'tomorrow is a new day with no mistakes in it.' I got that one from Anne of Green Gables, in case you're wondering, although I'd love to claim it as my own. Such an inspiring line, don't you think?

Each day, a brand-new start. A chance to do things better. To make things right.

Promise you'll come to see me straight after school. It is imperative I hug you.
~ H

The idea of wrapping his arms around the slender girl turned his muscles to melted marshmallow. A grin skittered over his lips as he nervously typed back.

Why?
~ T

Oh, Tristan. Don't you know?
Hugs are one of the most underrated acts of kindness on this earth. They make everything better, if only for a moment.
~ H

A smile tugged at his lips, pulling the right side of his face north.

Then I will most definitely be climbing through your window tomorrow afternoon.
Until then, sleep well, sweet Helena.
~ T

Sweet Helena—how can I not have the world's most charming dreams after being called that by a handsome knight?
~ H

He couldn't reply. Instead he ran his fingers over her words, his heart thumping a loud tune that he'd never heard before.

16

A Random Hug of Kindness

Tristan couldn't wait for the end of the day. A hug from Helena. It sounded so innocent, so sweet—so incredibly what he needed. His life had been tainted with so much bitterness and anger over the past two years, torn between two people who claimed to love him yet couldn't look past their own hurt to actually see him.

Helena, with her beguiling green eyes, was pure light, a rainbow after a storm. Maybe that was why he was so drawn to her.

Tristan bought a sandwich at lunchtime and headed

out to the bleachers to eat in peace. He didn't need the company; he could hang out with Helena and get his fill that afternoon.

The sun was vivid in the sky, making the white bleachers blinding. Tristan squinted, wishing he'd remembered his shades, but he wasn't about to complain. Spring was on its way and he was ready for the warmer weather. The freshly cut grass of the field was a vibrant green, the smell wafting up his nose and reminding him of summer ball games.

Plunking onto the second to top tier, Tristan yanked out his sandwich and quickly unwrapped it. He was about to take his first bite when he heard a faint sniff, then a shuddering breath, followed by a soft whimper.

He cringed, wondering if he could just ignore it, or maybe even sneak away without being noticed. That would be a really jerk thing to do though, and if it slipped out around Helena, she'd probably tell him off for being heartless.

With a sigh, he tucked his sandwich into his bag and bent down to peer between his legs. Beneath the bleachers, huddled against the side, was Mikayla. Her skinny arms were wrapped around her knees, clutching them to her chest like a teddy bear. Her face was red and blotchy, her freckles covered with wet tears.

Tristan's gut twisted uncomfortably, his reluctance turning his legs to lead. He glanced up, staring at the baseball diamond in the right-hand corner of the field. It'd be so easy to jump down and jog away, touch home plate and disappear back into the school, but...

Do the right thing, man.

Clenching his jaw, he snatched his bag, trotted down the stairs, and ducked beneath the bleachers.

"Hey," he said softly, easing onto the ground beside her.

"Hi." Her short word came out as a near squeak, tears making it hard for her to talk.

She slashed at them, sniffing and swallowing.

"What's up?" Tristan tipped to the side, lightly knocking her shoulder with his arm.

She shrugged, her chin trembling. "Oh, you know, just the usual. Owen trying to make my life hell."

Tristan sighed, anger and pity flittering through him. "What'd he do this time?"

"He posted a picture of me on Instagram and Facebook and Twitter and Tumblr! It's been doctored and makes me look like I'm naked in his bed." She swiped a finger under her nose. "He wrote a post about what we got up to, but it's all lies. I never slept with him! That's why we broke up. I wasn't ready and he got really pissed off with me, so I dumped him...and he won't let me forget it."

"He's such an asswipe." Tristan's voice cut through her tears, an angry whisper that made her laugh. It was a watery, pathetic sound. She nodded, a fresh wave of tears convulsing her body.

"I know I shouldn't care what anyone thinks, but he's kind of popular in this school and now he's got them believing we slept together. So the girls who like him hate me and the girls who hate him are disgusted with me.

Catcalls and whispered gossip have been following me all day." She sucked in a sob. "My mom's on Facebook. What if she sees it?"

"I'm sure they can take that kind of thing down. You could report it somehow."

She nodded. "Yeah, probably. I just hate that I even have to." Her words were punctured with breathy jerks, her stomach still spasming after her sob-fest.

"Hey." He nudged her softly. "You haven't done anything wrong. *He's* the asshole."

"Then why do I feel so dirty?" New tears flooded her eyes and she covered her face with her hands, a little whimper shooting out of her mouth.

Tristan didn't know what to say or how else to comfort her. He hated the sound of her tears. He wanted to pummel Owen into the ground for being such a dick, but he wouldn't. He didn't want to fight, especially if the fight wasn't his.

Mikayla rested her forehead against her knees, her small body still convulsing.

Hugs are one of the most underrated acts of kindness on this earth. They make everything better, if only for a moment.

Helena's sweet words whispered through his brain and before he could stop himself, he raised his arm and gently nestled it around Mikayla's shoulders. She leaned into his embrace, resting her head on his shoulder and whimpering again.

Tristan squeezed a little tighter, perching his chin on the top of her head and whispering, "Everything's going to be okay."

She nodded and pressed her face into his chest. Her arm snaked around his waist and she held on like her life depended on it. Tristan rubbed her back, not saying a word as her body jerked against him.

It was kind of nice holding her. She didn't smell like jasmine. Her hair had a citrus freshness to it, but her tiny arm around his waist, the way her head felt against his shoulder, that part was sweet. And the part that made it sweet was that Tristan was doing the right thing.

Mikayla's tears dried up, her quaking body stopped spasming, and after a while she went still in his arms. A light breeze snuck between the bleachers and ruffled Mikayla's fine hair. It tickled his chin and he leaned back, brushing the tendrils away.

"Thanks, Tristan," Mikayla whispered, squeezing his waist and sitting away from him. "Thanks for listening."

"Yeah, sure." He nodded.

An awkward silence landed on him and he twitched his lips, not sure what he was supposed to do.

The bell saved his life, beckoning them back to class. He jumped up, probably too quickly.

"Are you coming?"

"Yeah, in a minute." Her eyes were puffy and swollen, her nose still fire engine red.

He hitched his bag onto his shoulder and smiled down at her. "Maybe you should skip this period."

"I'll think about it." She shrugged, forcing a brief grin.

Tapping her boot with the toe of his shoe, he winked at her. "Don't worry. I'll cover for you."

"Thanks." A smile didn't reach her lips, but it brushed

her eyes for a second.

He ducked out from under the bleachers and walked away, unsure what else to do or say. It felt good knowing he'd done the right thing. He'd hoped it was enough. Sliding his hands into his pockets, he bobbed his head, smiling as he touched his foot on home plate.

Yeah, it was something.

It had been enough.

17

Romeo Rewritten

Covering for Mikayla was easy. The teacher bought his lie about her feeling unwell without even batting an eyelid. Curious stares followed him to his seat, as per usual, but he held his head high, unflustered by them. He'd done the right thing and damn, if it didn't make him feel good. He couldn't wait to tell Helena.

He biked home from school in record time, dumping his bike and backpack next to his father's car and racing across the grass. He didn't think to check the trellis or the fact that each time he climbed it, it grew a little weaker.

All he could think about was reaching Helena, stepping into her embrace and feeling her arms wrap around him. Jasmine would envelop him and he'd be lost and found all in the same moment.

Stretching high, he reached for his normal spot on the trellis, throwing his weight into it and sucking in his breath when it snapped. His foot slipped and he gripped the other side, swinging around. He crashed into the wall, his arm twisting painfully. Without meaning to, he glanced down, a sudden vertigo seizing him.

"Tristan!" Helena's sweet voice caught his attention and he looked up in time to see her throwing down a blanket.

He grinned, swinging himself back around and capturing the "rope." With a grunt, he pulled himself up, his arm muscles straining when he neared the top. Helena's hand gripped his jacket, helping to haul him through the window. He landed in a heap, chuckling and slapping the floor before rolling over to face her.

"Thank you, Rapunzel."

She giggled, flicking her long locks over her shoulder and pulling in the blanket. "I saw you coming and when I heard the snap, I acted without a second thought."

"Well, thank—"

A creak on the stairs made Helena gasp. Throwing the bundled blanket at him, she spun him around and shoved him towards the clothes rack at the side of the room.

He didn't argue with her, just stepped behind the clothes and held his breath as the door banged open.

"Helena, did you hear something outside?" The uptight dragon snapped out the words.

Helena's sweet tenor was in utter contrast. "Outside?"

"I thought I heard something breaking. You haven't been opening the windows again, have you?"

"It's a warm day today. I have had the windows open."

Her mother sighed and Tristan listened to her quick steps on the wooden floor.

"Maybe it was a bird." Helena looked over her shoulder. Tristan could see her twinkling smile between the puffy princess dress and the thick coat hanging from the rack.

"Hmmmm, well, it'll be cold soon enough, so let's close this for now, shall we?"

The window snapped down in one swift movement.

"Yes, Mother."

"What are you wearing, my dear?" Her mother's voice was low and strained.

Helena giggled, although Tristan could tell it was forced. "Oh you know me, just playing pretend."

There was a pregnant pause.

Tristan craned his neck and spied through the clothes as Helena's mother gently touched her daughter's puffy sleeve and murmured, "Sweet child."

Helena smiled, looking as innocent and endearing as her mother no doubt saw her.

The woman blinked, crossing her arms and turning for the door. "I'm just preparing dinner. I'll call you when it's time to come down."

"Okay."

Tristan waited for the clip of retreating shoes before sneaking out of hiding. Helena spun to face him, patting her chest with a sweet laugh. Her overwhelming relief was obvious, which confused Tristan a little. The woman who had just called Helena *sweet child* seemed weak and non-threatening, more likely to crumple into a ball of tears than scorch him with fiery flames.

"What would she do if she caught me in here?" He frowned, stepping over the trunk of dress-ups by the clothes rack.

"I'm not sure, but let's *never* find out." Helena winked, her smile glittering.

Tristan gazed at her cherry-red cheeks before taking in her silky, powder blue princess dress. It had a large scoop neck, puffy sleeves, and a fitted bodice that highlighted the curve of her small breasts and tiny waist before billowing out at the hips. She looked like that girl from the Cinderella movie.

"Uh, what—what are you wearing?"

"Oh." Helena held the plush skirt out, doing a little curtsy. "I am Juliet."

He frowned, his head jerking back in surprise.

She stood straight, bouncing on her tiptoes. "I'm playing pretend, Tristan."

He bit the inside of his cheek, a flush of embarrassment and bemusement coursing through him. "I thought only kids played pretend."

Her hands landed on her hips and she rocked back on her heels. "Why should there be an age restriction? Actors do it all the time."

"Yeah, but..." He pointed at her dress, finding it hard to argue.

"And since I'll never make it to Hollywood, I guess I'll just have to do it here." Her sweet chuckle made Tristan smile. "I thought I'd pretend to be Juliet for you. Let's bring some life into that play and make you fall in love."

Her dress rustled as she skipped over to the coffee table and grabbed the open book resting on it.

"*O Romeo, Romeo! Wherefore art thou Romeo? Deny thy father and refuse thy name; Or, if thou wilt not, be but sworn my love, and I'll no longer be a Capulet.*" She raised her arm with a flourish, giving him a pointed look as though she wanted him to say the next line.

Tristan's eyebrows puckered. "Um...I don't think we're up to that part yet."

"Oh, but it's my favorite part of the play. Do it with me anyway, please? I swear you'll fall in love."

Heat kissed his skin and he scratched the back of his neck, glancing at the floor. "Helena, the play is totally depressing. Putting on fancy clothes and reading it with you isn't going to make it better. They both die."

The book slaps against her legs as she drops her arms with an exasperated eye roll. "Yes, because they love each other so much."

"Why does the world always have to be tainted with sadness? Why can't couples just stay together for...forever?" he croaked, humiliation at his outburst forcing his gaze to remain on the floor.

Silk slippers padded over to him, coming into his line of sight and stopping by his feet. Helena's cool fingers touched his cheek, her caress soft and delicious.

"Oh, Tristan, you have such a tender heart." Wrapping her arms around his neck, she pulled him into an embrace. Jasmine surrounded him, dancing up his nostrils while her hair tickled his cheek. Sliding his arms around her thin waist, he spread his hands along her back and gathered her to him, the puffs of fabric crinkling against his legs. He closed his eyes and breathed her in, relishing her sweetness.

He could have stayed like that for the rest of the day, but she pulled back, holding him at arm's length and grinning. "We shall just have to rewrite the ending." She winked, stepping back and holding out her hand. "Come, Tristan, join me. Be my prince?"

He cringed, awkward embarrassment getting the better of him.

She giggled, snatching his hand and pulling him towards the dress-up rack. Hangers flicked across the beam—*slide, click, slide, click.*

"Nope. Nope. Maybe. Not quite." She stopped, her face lighting with a radiant smile as she pulled out a velvet jacket with long tails and gold embroidery. "Yes."

A feeble whine escaped his throat, making Helena giggle again.

"Just don't make me wear tights." He grimaced, sliding off his jacket and letting her hitch the coat onto his shoulders.

"It fits you well." She tugged on the sleeves and did one little yank at the back before spinning him around and nodding her approval.

He wriggled his shoulders, still feeling like a fool as he looked down at the ridiculous attire.

"Come, my Romeo. Let us rewrite history."

She strode away from him, moving into the open part of the room and spinning on her heel. "So, let's skip forward to the end scene and pretend that Juliet awakens in the tomb and sees Romeo lying dead." Skipping over to him, Helena took his arm and steered him towards the couch. Once his knees were pressed against the arm, she gave his chest a light shove and he flailed backwards.

"Well, that was a little ungainly." She made a face that Tristan could only roll his eyes at. "Oh, come on." She slapped his knee. "Play my game."

Fighting a grin, Tristan shuffled on the cushions, laying his hands on his chest and closing his eyes.

"That's better. Now, where are we?"

Tristan peeked one eye open to see Helena flicking through to the back of the book.

"Ah, here we go." Pulling her shoulders back, she cleared her throat and looked at him.

He snapped his eyes shut before he got scolded.

"*What's here? a cup, closed in my true love's hand?*" Helena stopped and tutted. "Oh, we forgot a cup. Blast it. Just pretend to hold one."

Tristan's lips twitched with a grin but he did as he was told, rounding his fingers around an invisible stem.

"Hang on." He popped his eyes open and sat up. "Hasn't Romeo had the poison by now? Shouldn't we be going back to the part where he sees Juliet pretending to be dead?"

"*I'm* rewriting this version and I like Juliet's lines here, so please, have a little faith. Magic is afoot." She grinned.

With a confused frown, Tristan laid back down, closing his eyes as commanded.

Helena's skirts rustled as she approached him and perched on the edge of the sofa. Her hand was light on his chest, her soft fingers trailing down to his hands.

"*Poison, I see, hath been his timeless end,*" she whispered. "*O churl! drunk all, and left no friendly drop to help me after? I will kiss thy lips.*"

Tristan sucked in a quick inaudible breath, willing his eyes to remain closed as he listened to the rustle of fabric move against the sofa. Her upper body pressed into his chest. Tristan swallowed, picturing the curve of her breasts as she leaned on top of him. Her warm breath tickled his chin and her finger glided down his cheek, whispering over the corner of his mouth.

"For 'tis in my lips that magic dwells."

Tristan held his breath, listening to Helena's new lines.

"We are but star-crossed lovers, destined to endure the ages. Our love cannot be broken. It cannot die and so I kiss thee, fair Romeo, and awaken you from untimely slumber."

Her lips were soft, a fleeting brush of tender skin against his own. They tasted sweet, like berries. He wanted to move, to place his hand on her head and force her to linger, but he couldn't breathe. He'd kissed girls before, but never magic. He'd never kissed magic.

"*Thy lips are warm,*" Helena whispered.

Tristan opened his eyes, his gaze crashing into hers as she searched his face, a look of awestruck wonder dancing in her eyes.

He smiled, more of a feeling than a lip movement. Pulling his hand from beneath her, he gently laid it on the back of her head.

"Juliet, my love," he whispered.

She smiled, her eyes dancing like sugar plum fairies. He was about to pull her back down so their lips could meet again, but a creaking on the stairs jerked them apart.

Helena gasped, jumping off him. Panic washed over her face as she flung her arms in the air and mouthed, "Hide!"

Flipping over the back of the sofa, he caught himself before crashing onto the floor, gently easing onto the wood and snatching his hand out of view as the door flew open.

"Helena, it's time for you to set the table. Get changed now. Dinner will be soon."

"Of course, Mother." Helena's words were pinched and edgy. Tristan grimaced, hoping her mother wouldn't notice.

He remained a statue on the floor, pressing his fingers into the wood and trying not to breathe.

"Are you all right? You look flushed."

Helena's laugh was breathy and all telling. "Just my imagination...dreaming of a true love's kiss."

The silent pause that followed felt raw and icy. Tristan pressed his ear to the wooden boards, trying to peek beneath the sofa, but all he could see were a pair of pale blue ballet slippers next to a black pair of well-worn pumps.

Helena cleared her throat. "I'll be down in just a moment."

"All right." Her mother's voice sounded small and insignificant. "We're having shepherd's pie."

"Oh, one of my favorites. Thank you."

An awkward silence followed and then the dragon was gone, the stairs creaking out her departure.

Breathing out a sigh of relief, Tristan scrambled off the floor and moved over to Helena, resting his fingers lightly on her lower back. "I guess I should get out of here."

"I wish you didn't have to." She pouted, her eyes large with sorrow.

Tristan smiled, turning her to face him and brushing his fingers down the curve of her cheek. "I'll come back."

Her lips rose with a smile and he stepped away, shrugging out of his jacket and grabbing his bag out of hiding. He wanted to thank her for the kiss, the drama, and the fact that she'd made him look like a fool and he kind of hadn't minded. But he couldn't voice any of that, so instead he took her hand and raised it to his lips.

"Good night, my lady." He kissed her knuckles and gave her a charming smile.

She giggled. "Good night, my prince. I shall count the hours until your return."

With that, he climbed out the window, feeling like a knight of the realm as he descended the trellis, taking care to avoid the weak spot. He landed in the grass and stared back up the tower, blowing a kiss at the closed window before spinning on his heel and practically skipping back towards the fence.

18

Classical Music in a Fairytale Castle

From that day on, Helena's attic became a regular hangout for Tristan. Every day after school, he'd climb the tower to play pretend, and to chat about everything from music to history to books to their theories on the world. Some days they did homework together; other times they sat beside one another reading. Helena's stories often drew Tristan to her side when she read aloud brilliant lines that captured her. She'd snuggle into his chest, her long hair cascading over his knees as he gazed over her shoulder at the text. Her jasmine scent would waft around him and the weight of her body on his would fill his heart with a languid contentment he'd never thought possible.

Every now and then they bickered about silly things that didn't matter. But most of the time they laughed, they smiled, and Helena's collection of hanging cranes continued to grow.

"Let me teach you how to make one." She beckoned him towards her desk one sunny afternoon when the light danced in her flaxen hair, turning the long locks into a trail of silken gold.

He ambled across the room, straining for noises on the stairwell before taking a seat.

"Don't worry." Helena patted his arm. "She's down in her room listening to 'Brahms's Symphony No. 1.' Every year, on this exact date, she is consumed by that symphony."

"Why?" Tristan sat down and took the sheet of paper Helena passed him, noting the way her face flickered with a sad smile.

"It was the music she was listening to when she met my father." Helena's cheeks rose, her eyes lighting with a dreamy smile. "When she was at university, she used to travel every holiday. She'd take her classical music with her wherever she went and wander the castles and ruins of Europe engrossed in melody and history and her own imagination."

Helena folded her sheet of paper diagonally, pointing at Tristan's sheet. He copied her, creasing the paper with his nail.

"Now do it the opposite way." She unfolded the sheet and did a new fold.

Tristan followed suit. "So, your mom would just walk around with her headphones on?"

"Yes." Helena giggled, unfolding her paper and making two more creases until she had a sheet with eight segments. "She'd chosen Brahms because she was in Germany and he was a German composer. She was working her way through them as she toured the country."

"And where did your parents meet?"

Helena let out a wistful sigh, leaning her elbow against the desk and resting her chin on her hand.

"She was roaming the grounds of Hohenzollern Castle. It's this spellbinding place in Germany. A castle where fairytales are created." Her smile slipped for a second, her lips flirting with a frown before she could catch it. Sitting straight, she focused back on her sheet of paper. "Now, turn it over and fold like this."

Tristan watched her make the folds until she was left with a little square. The tip of his tongue peeked out the corner of his mouth as he concentrated, trying to fold it the same way.

"That's it." Helena stepped in, helping him line up the paper before he pressed it flat.

Tristan studied her, his gaze trying to unearth another nugget of truth...figure out why she was fighting a frown.

"You want to go there one day, don't you?" he asked.

She shrugged, folding the edges of the paper so they made a kite shape. She glanced at him and nodded at the paper. With a little sigh, Tristan copied her, his gaze flicking to her face as he worked. She bit her lips together, blinking a few times and refusing to look his way.

"And then like this." She did the next few folds quickly and he had to race to keep up. He fumbled and she had to stop and show him once more. He rectified his mistake, creasing the paper so it sat flat like hers.

They worked in silence for a few more minutes, Tristan trying to figure out how to get her talking. He usually couldn't keep her quiet when it came to storytelling and castles. Her sealed lips were unnerving.

She lifted the bird and showed him the final move. "Now you just pull the wings, like so...but not too hard or they'll rip."

Tristan delicately spread the wings, a smile appearing as he held up the bird.

"You did it." She grinned, clapping her hands and then clasping them together.

He snickered at her cuteness before looking back at his bird. "Yeah, and I think I'll need to do it a hundred more times before I memorize how to fold it."

She rested her head against his shoulder. "I'm happy to show you again."

He placed the bird down next to hers, resting the wings against each other. "Tell me the rest of the story," he whispered. "About your parents."

Her fingers trailed down his arm, skimming the fine dark hairs. "She was standing there, looking out at the view, music filling her mind. She was oblivious to the people around her, until my father appeared. Out of the corner of her eye, she saw him walk past and she said she stopped breathing. She'd never believed in love at first sight before...until she saw him."

Helena's fingers spread over the back of his hand, dipping between his knuckles. He squeezed his fingers, capturing hers within his.

"And then what happened?"

Helena perched her chin on his shoulder, her breath tickling the side of his neck. "Apparently my father caught her staring and stopped in his tracks. His face washed with a look of wonder and he stepped towards her and said, '*Hear my soul speak. The very instant I saw you, did my heart fly to your service.*'"

"And she bought that?" Tristan made a face, his cynical chuckle breathy and dry.

Helena shot back, her mouth agape, "For certain! Any man who says something that romantic owns your heart immediately." She squeezed his hand. "Poetry is made from love. It inspires love, and my parents are proof of that. Their hearts were fused that day and their souls will live together forever...in paradise."

Tristan swallowed, holding back his true thoughts on the matter. Love wasn't always made to last forever. There was no paradise for his parents. Maybe his father should have had some poetry up his sleeve.

Tristan skimmed his finger down the curve of her cheek. "So, that line your father said, what's that from?"

"Shakespeare, of course." Helena grinned and nestled her head back on his shoulder. "It's from *The Tempest*. My father's favorite play."

"You really are a thespian family, aren't you?"

"I know it must seem odd sometimes, like we've never really fit into this world. But there's magic in words and storytelling. I'd be lost without books, Tristan. They've kept me afloat through my darkest days. Escaping into another world full of love, enchantment...heroes. It keeps me breathing."

Lifting his shoulder, he gently encouraged Helena to move. She turned to look at him and he cupped her cheek. "The real world is full of those things too."

"But the good guys don't always win." Helena's forehead bunched, her mouth looking small and childlike when she frowned.

Tristan traced his thumb across her lower lip. "Sometimes they do."

She looked straight into his eyes, a dancing wonder making her own sparkle like emeralds. Sitting straight, she reached for her paper crane and collected a pen out of her stationery container.

"Tristan made his first paper crane today," Helena murmured as she wrote, "and made me believe that maybe fairytales can come true."

Tristan chuckled, his shoulders shaking. Popping the lid on, she went to put the pen back, but he snatched it out of her hand before she could. Taking off the lid, he pulled his own crane towards himself and wrote on the wing.

"I folded my first paper crane today," he said, "and Helena made me believe that poetry can win a girl's heart. Must learn some poetry."

Helena's laughter tinkled in the air. Placing the pen back, she flicked her hair over her shoulder and leaned her cheek against her hand, gazing at Tristan with unchecked affection.

"Oh, but you know so much already. You've been studying Shakespeare. You have a full armada of poetry up your sleeve. Now you just need to use it." She winked.

Clearing his throat, he straightened, puffing out his chest and lifting his chin.

"Sweet Helena, *this bud of love, by summer's*...something about breath and then a flower?"

Helena tipped back her head, laughter ringing true. Sitting forward, she rested her hand on his cheek, ready to say something, but then she paused. Her eyes searched his, her thumb caressing the corner of his left eye.

"Oh, Tristan, your eyes are a brilliant blue today."

Resting his hand on her waist, he trailed it down to her hip and gave it a gentle squeeze.

"Because of you," he whispered, leaning forward and kissing her.

19

An Excellent Tutor

Tristan adjusted his jeans, yanking them down at the knee and sticking out his foot while he waited for Miss Warren to hand back their Shakespeare assignments. He felt nervous for reasons he couldn't fathom. Maybe it was because he actually tried pretty hard on it, something he hadn't done for a long time, or maybe it was the fact that Helena had helped him and he wanted to make her proud.

The rustle of papers being flipped and turned followed by beaming smiles, frowns, and indifferent shrugs waffled through the classroom.

Placing the assignment on his desk, Miss Warren rested her hand on his shoulder and murmured in his ear, "See me after class, please."

Her voice was slightly chilly and a rock-hard stone dropped into his stomach. With a disappointed tut, he lifted the pages and thumbed through to the final grading page.

A+ was written in red on the top right corner.

His mouth popped open, his face bunching with confusion. Glancing over at Miss Warren, she caught his gaping stare and had to bite back her smile.

"Okay, class, let's go over what you'll need to prepare for your test on Monday." She clapped her hands and drew all eyes her way.

At the end of the lesson, Tristan packed up slowly, shuffling towards the front desk and waiting until the final student had walked out the door before raising his eyebrows at Miss. Warren. She sat at her desk, her slender arms folded and resting against the shiny black edge.

"Congratulations on such a great assignment."

"Thank you," he murmured, finding her stern look disconcerting.

"You know, for a guy who hates Shakespeare, you did surprisingly well. Is the work actually yours?"

Tristan's eyes bulged, his head bobbing before words could reach his mouth. "Yeah, yeah, of course it is."

She leaned back in her seat, looking skeptical. Her high cheekbones protruded while her eyes narrowed with scrutiny.

He scratched the back of his neck and gave it a squeeze.

"Cheating is not tolerated at this school, Mr. Parker. Now I'm not accusing you of plagiarism, but I find it very hard to believe that a student with your lack of enthusiasm can suddenly do so well. Who helped you with this? Did someone do it for you?"

He clenched his jaw, still gazing at the floor and rubbing the back of his neck.

"I really don't want to have to take this to Principal Smyth, but I won't have dishonesty in my class. It's not fair to me or your fellow students."

Giving in with a sigh, Tristan looked to the ceiling. "I had help. The assignment's mine, I swear, but I did have someone tutor me through it. She gave me a lot of great ideas and really helped me understand the play." His lips twitched. "She kind of brought it to life."

He glanced at his teacher, pleased with the sudden shift in her demeanor. Her deep brown gaze had softened to a rich nutmeg, her lips curving up at the edges.

"You're blushing," she murmured.

He cringed, flashing her a strained smile.

Her chuckle was sweet and melodic. "Is she a student at this school?"

"No, she's uh...homeschooled." Tristan cleared his throat and swallowed.

"Well, I'd love to meet her sometime." Miss Warren leaned forward again, threading her fingers together. "If she can get that kind of work out of you, I'd love to see what she could share with your classmates."

Tristan's nose wrinkled. "Yeah, she's a bit of a homebody."

"Ah." Miss Warren nodded. "The shy type."

He nodded, finding that an easier solution than delving into the weird drama of Helena's life.

Miss Warren pressed her hands against her desk and slowly stood. "Okay, well, I'm glad you're not cheating and that you've found yourself an inspiring tutor. Maybe she can help you study this weekend."

Tristan frowned. "Unfortunately, I'm at my mom's this weekend." His shoulder hitched. "She's picking me up at six."

"Then I suggest you make the most of your afternoon." Miss Warren winked, an amused smile resting on her lips. "See you on Monday, Mr. Parker."

"See ya." He raised his hand and shot out the door, feeling like he'd dodged a bullet. Running through the busy traffic, he skipped his locker and loped down the stairs to his bike, anxious to show Helena his assignment.

"I like this line," Helena nudged Tristan's leg with the toe she had tucked beneath him. "*A good explanation of the emotional journey these characters go through. Deep insights and a clear understanding of Shakespeare's underlying message.*"

Tristan blushed, crossing his arms and nodding. "That

was all you. No wonder she thought I was cheating."

Helena leaned forward, gripping his arm and shaking her head. "It wasn't just me. You came up with this too. All I did was steer you in the right direction, and you made all the correct assumptions." She grinned, leaning back and hugging the assignment to her chest. "I'm so proud of you."

He brushed the air with his hand, his cheeks heating with color.

Helena laid the assignment in her lap and smoothed out the crinkles. Tristan wondered if he should mention the test, but ignored Miss Warren's advice. He didn't want to waste the few minutes he had left studying. He just wanted to hang out, bask in Helena's sunshine.

"We should write a play, you and me." Her sweet voice tickled the air, her words taking him by surprise.

"A play?" His dark eyebrows dipped together.

"Yes." She giggled. "Or a story. It could be fun."

"What would it be about?"

Looking up with a sigh, Helena rested her head against the back of the sofa. "Two people, divided by an ocean of green grass and a towering castle. Two lost souls who find themselves in each other." Her head popped back up. "What do you think?"

"You are such a romantic." His voice was dry, but he couldn't stop his smile in time.

"Oh, come on, you love that about me."

"I do." He hesitated for only a second before leaning towards her. She met him halfway with a glimmering smile, clutching the front of his shirt as they pressed their lips together.

Tristan wanted to deepen the kiss, taste the edge of her sweet, red tongue, but he didn't have the courage to dive in. He didn't want to scare her off. She was so sweet and innocent, so untouched by the world. He kind of liked that about her.

"So, what's your idea, then?" She rested her hand on his neck, searching his face with her dancing eyes.

"My idea? Hmmm." He pursed his lips. "How about a girl who is trapped in a tower and a handsome, brave, good-looking knight"—she giggled—"comes to rescue her. They climb out the window and gallop away on his trusty steed to explore the world and all it has to offer."

The dancing light in Helena's eyes died away, replaced with a cool glare. "How many times do we have to have this conversation, Tristan? You know I can never leave with you."

The light, airy feeling in the room vanished, snapped away as the serious conversation reared its head again.

"Your mother needs help. You're doing her no favors by staying locked up in here." He ran his hand down her arm.

"How would I ever get her help?" She swatted his hand away, crossing her arms. "She won't leave the house. She can barely open the door for the delivery man without having a panic attack."

"Hence the reason she needs help."

"Tristan." She closed her eyes. "Please don't."

Not wanting to taint their last few minutes together, Tristan pressed his lips into a straight line and reached for her hand, gently threading their fingers together. "I just hate the idea that we have an expiration date."

"One that's at least a year away. You don't even know what you want to do with your life anyway. You very well could be here for years to come."

"I'm not spending the rest of my life waiting on my father. I'm not..." He sighed. "I can't stay forever."

"Then I guess you better start training him to look after himself." Her eyebrows rose, making her look like a governess who'd had lemon juice for breakfast.

"I'm trying," Tristan muttered darkly. It was a lie. He wasn't training anyone. It was easier just to do it himself. Helena had a point. It'd only make things difficult when he went to leave, but still. He wasn't staying with his dad for the rest of eternity. He also couldn't spend his adult years climbing a tower.

"You need to stop worrying about the future and live in the now or you'll miss everything." Helena spoke softly, glancing at her paper cranes.

He looked at her with an irritated scowl. "How can you say that to me when you're not doing that yourself?"

"How am I not doing it?" She tried to wriggle her fingers free but he tightened his grip.

"You're trapped inside a house. You're not living—you're existing."

"I'll have you know that I have traveled the world in my mind," she snapped. "I have seen things that you can't even imagine. I have lived in every age and I have laughed and smiled and felt more happiness in this house than you probably *ever* have. What does the world outside have to offer me that I can't get in the safety of my own home?" Her eyes flared a brilliant green.

He caressed the back of her hand with his thumb. "Let me take you out and show you."

With a pinched expression, she wriggled her fingers loose and sighed. "You know I can't do that. If anything bad happened she wouldn't survive it."

Tristan ran a hand through his hair and sighed, his lungs deflating as he once again lost the battle.

"Well?"

"Well, what?" He looked at her with a frown.

She raised her finger, pointing at the open window behind him. "Aren't you going to get up and storm out that window like you normally do when we have this quarrel?"

The edge of his mouth twitched, a half smile daring to show. Clearing his throat, he drew in a slow breath, plucked the assignment off her lap, and started rereading Miss Warren's glowing comments.

Out of the corner of his eye, he saw Helena's face rise with a grin, her bottom teeth brushing over her lower lip before she lifted the book off the coffee table and resumed reading.

Fifteen minutes later, a car horn beeped in Tristan's driveway. He shot from his seat and peered out the window.

"She's early," he muttered.

"The sooner you go, the sooner you return." Helena's hand rested on his back, between his shoulder blades.

"I just can't be bothered doing another weekend,

trying to explain why I'm not playing ball anymore. Not to mention putting up with Curtis and his saffron. I should have just put her off."

"You promised you wouldn't. She's your mother. If she had her way you'd be living with her permanently. As it is, she only gets to see you twice a month. Think how that must make her feel."

"Yeah, yeah, I know." Tristan sighed.

Helena rested her chin on his shoulder and chuckled in his ear. "Just be honest with her, and remember that I'm only an email away."

He spun around, pulling her against him and kissing the side of her head. "I'll come over as soon as I get back."

"I'll be waiting for you." Her smile was divine.

He quickly pecked her lips before scrambling out the window. Glancing at her face one last time, he carefully descended the tower, a light breeze rippling through his clothing as he imagined his return.

"*Parting is such sweet sorrow,*" he murmured as he landed on the ground and crossed the ocean of grass with a dreamy smile.

20

A Fair Maiden to the Rescue

His mother's car had been freshly cleaned. The dashboard was dust-free, the carpets beneath his feet plush from a recent vacuuming. It was a far cry from his dad's old pickup truck. Shuffling down in his seat, he went to rest his foot on the dash, but a sharp glance from his mother had his foot landing back on the floor.

A smile brushed his lips as he imagined he was speeding along in a black carriage with the Wicked Witch of the West. She had kidnapped him and was dragging him south to her evil lair where Doctor Curt-bum was preparing a bubbling cauldron of saffron-infused poison.

He chuckled.

"What is it?" His mother's voice was sharp.

He shook his head, tugging on his beanie and looking out the window. He caught his mother's frown and eye roll out of the corner of his eye but ignored it, instead diving back into his imagination and having a blast.

As soon as they arrived at the house, he mumbled a greeting to Curtis and disappeared into his room, typing up his story in an email to Helena.

He wasn't able to check his inbox until after an awkward dinner filled with stilted conversation and painful wedding talk. Curtis wanted Tristan to be a groomsman.

Was he out of his mind?

Tristan didn't even want to go to the wedding.

As soon as the dishes were rinsed, Tristan made a beeline for his computer. Closing his bedroom door, he turned on the lamp and tapped the space bar as soon as he sat down. The screen came to life. An instant grin popped onto his face when he saw the red little circle on his Mail icon.

My dear Tristan,

I adore the premise of your story. Your two villains are quite captivating. I'm also rather fond of the fair maiden who comes to rescue you.

Hope fluttered in Tristan's chest, his airways

restricting until he read the next paragraph and slumped into his chair.

Let us give her a flying horse, much like Pegasus, although I want hers to be chocolate brown with a white patch on his left eye. His wingspan will be intimidating and he will fly at the speed of light.
~ H xx

Tristan's lips twitched as he typed a message back.

Things have gotten worse for the victim. Come this summer, he will be forced to don a suit that will make him look like a penguin. He will be pranced around in front of lords and ladies— a pet monkey on display—while the evil doctor and his mistress get married.
Help, my sweet Helena. How will you rescue me?
~ T xxx

I will rescue you by charging in, sword ablaze and demanding (very politely, of course) that the captors hand over my prince or I shall have to slay them both where they stand.
~ H xxxx

Tristan chuckled, picturing her upon a horse, yelling at Curtis and his mother while they hovered in the kitchen. His fingers were poised to type back when a new message appeared.

In all seriousness though, why don't you just talk to them? You could always tell them you don't want to be part of the wedding.
~ H xxxxx

He swallowed, the idea of that much honesty cutting his air supply short. He tapped his index finger on the keys, picturing the conversation for a moment. His lip curled and he shook his head, typing back:

I can't do that. My mother would flip out. She already hates that I chose Dad. If I don't go to the wedding, she'll be crushed. I can't do that to her. I may not agree with <u>any</u> of her choices, but I can't hurt her like that. Like you said, she is my mother.
~ T xxxxx

She is, and I understand exactly where you're coming from.
Don't be afraid to say how you feel though. It might help set you free.
~ H xxxxxx

I'm not trapped in a tower. I can leave whenever I like.
~ T xxxxxxx

She didn't reply to his final email. There were no more growing lines of kisses, just a dead silence that told him she wasn't willing to go there again. He probably shouldn't have sent it. There was no winning the argument with her. He couldn't free someone who wanted to stay trapped. Just like she couldn't help someone who didn't want it, and he couldn't make two oblivious lovers understand how much damage they'd caused.

Slumping back with a sigh, Tristan waited another ten minutes before closing his laptop and heading back into the living area.

His mother was watching *Castle*—her favorite detective show—so he sat down beside her and lost himself to a world of crime fighting in an attempt to forget about his stubborn girl and the hopeless situation they were both stuck in.

The rest of the weekend went smoothly. Quietly, but smoothly.

Tristan's leg bobbed like a jackhammer as they drove north. He'd missed Helena, hated not having her just next door, knowing he could sneak up and see her whenever he liked.

A hot blush kissed his cheeks as he gazed out the window and smiled.

He was so whipped.

"So, do you have a big week at school?"

Mom had already asked him that. They'd exhausted all small talk within the first twenty-four hours of his visit. Since Tristan wasn't willing to give them much more, the rest of the time had been filled with wedding chatter. He'd silently endured it, not complaining but not smiling either.

"It's not too bad. I have a few assignments looming and a couple of tests, but no exams yet."

"Have you—?"

He glanced at her, noting the way her cheekbones protruded as she hesitated over her question.

"Have I what?"

His mother smiled, her right shoulder hitching. "You just seem a little happier. Still really quiet, but you're smiling, freely almost, and I'm... I was wondering if you've met someone...or joined a sports team again?"

It was an effort to keep a straight face. The woman seriously did not give up.

Tristan licked his lips, fighting his grin and going for what he hoped looked like a casual nod.

"I think I'm just finding my way, feeling more settled. I haven't picked up baseball again yet. But you know, I'm not actually missing it."

Her expression was pensive, but he could see her battle to keep it that way. She cleared her throat. "I'm so surprised by that. You were obsessed as a kid."

He shrugged. "People change. I've kind of lost my love of the game."

Her face crested with sadness, and she blinked rapidly while looking at the road ahead.

"Don't be sad. I've—I've found new things to fall in love with." He smiled at her. "I got an A+ on my latest English assignment."

"Really? Wow! That's great, sweetie." She flashed him a grin, but it was fleeting, soon swallowed back and replaced with a sad smile that hit him in the chest. "I'm so glad you're happy," she whispered.

He opened his mouth, closing it again when his courage failed him. Soon the only sound in the car was the turning of wheels beneath them, the smooth hum as they sped north along the main highway.

Tristan kept glancing at his mother, her strained expression making her wrinkles show. Her knuckles were white as she gripped the wheel, the ridiculous rock Curtis had given her glinting in the afternoon sunlight.

Tristan looked away from it, the muscles in his jaw working overtime. Finally he let out a soft huff and turned back to her.

"You know, I—" He sighed and licked his lower lip. "I hate what you did to Dad...to our family. You lied, and you cheated. I'm sure you had your reasons, but whatever they were, what you did was wrong."

She whipped to face him, staring at him with wide eyes before remembering she was driving and turning back to face the road. Her skin was white, her lips trembling.

Tristan pursed his lips and shrugged. "But I don't hate *you*...and I didn't choose Dad because of what you did. You've been trying to win me over ever since the day you started cheating and it's getting kind of old."

Her expression buckled, lines lacing her face as she fought a sudden onset of tears.

"Why did you choose your father?" She choked out

the words.

"Because you had someone to come home to." Tristan swallowed. "And he didn't."

Her lips wobbled, making a funny shape before she pulled them back into line. "I always thought you were trying to punish me."

He scoffed, shaking his head and staring down at his shoes. "Not to be harsh, Mom, but only narcissists think that way."

Her lips parted, a quick scowl surfacing before scuttling into hiding behind a sorrowful frown. "Just as long as you're happy," she finally murmured. "That's all that matters to me."

Gazing at her with the best smile he could muster, he nodded. "I am. I'm really happy."

She met his smile with one of her own and the thick fog that had been pushing the car into the road lifted. Tristan sat up straight, feeling the effects of it. The lightness was helped along by the giddy bubbles popping in his belly, reminding him that very soon he'd be wrapping himself around a shining light that smelled like jasmine and tasted like summer-berry lip gloss.

21

Summer-berry Lips

Much to Tristan's relief, his mother dropped him and left, not bothering to come into the house and start a fight like the last couple of times. Tristan raised his hand and waved her off, waiting until she was down the road before bolting inside.

His father was on the couch in his usual spot, feet on the coffee table, beer in hand.

"Hey, Dad." He brushed past him, taking a cursory glance at the screen and noting the Yankees were set to win the game. Tristan rushed up the stairs to dump his stuff and get over to Helena's place. Skipping back down, he smiled at his father when he glanced over his shoulder.

"How was it?" His dad turned away from the game, his smile slightly bemused. "You catch up with some of your old friends or something? There was that girl, wasn't there? What was her name again?"

"No, Dad. I didn't see my old friends." Tristan chuckled, clearing his throat and forcing his lips to behave.

"What's up with you lately?"

"What do you mean?" He checked his expression, hoping it was sitting bland and even.

His dad shrugged, swiveling back to the TV and taking another swig from his bottle.

"So, I'm just gonna go for a walk." Tristan pointed over his shoulder as he walked backwards into the kitchen.

His dad paused, the beer halfway to his lips. "O-kay."

"To get dinner stuff." Tristan pushed up his sleeves.

"Cool." He couldn't see his father's face but took his head nodding as a license to skip out. His dad never usually asked where he was going or what he was up to. He could probably tell him the truth and he still wouldn't mind, but Helena was Tristan's secret and he wasn't about to change that. He just had to remember to run to the store before coming home. A can of soup and a loaf of fresh bread would have to do for dinner.

"I'll see you soon," he called, racing out the back door.

He was tapping on Helena's window within ten minutes. Her long braid flicked down her back as she jumped up and ran across the room. She lifted the window quickly, helping him in and wrapping her arms around him before he'd even had a chance to stand straight.

"I know it was only two days, but I missed you," she whispered against his shoulder.

Tristan closed his eyes with a relieved sigh, gliding his arms around her waist and pulling her close. She giggled when he lifted her off the ground, the sweet sound kissing the side of his neck. Placing her back down, he let her go and lightly held her face, his thumbs brushing the edge of her jaw. He could drown in the turquoise oasis of her gaze. Her eyes were a deep spring, reflecting the stars of a brilliant night sky.

She smiled, her white teeth straight and perfect, her pointy sweet nose wrinkling between her eyes.

Words were lost to him. He was sucked in by her beauty—the glossy sparkle on her lips, the tender way she drank him in. He leaned toward her, stopping a quarter inch from her lips and breathing in the jasmine swirling around him. She always did this to him, put his senses into overdrive, intoxicating him and turning his mind to putty.

His eyelids fluttered closed, her warm, tickling breath wrenching him in and closing the space between them. Her summer-berry lips consumed him. He lightly gripped the back of her neck, increasing the pressure. Before he could stop it, the tip of his tongue snuck out for a proper taste. Her fingers curled into his shirt as he brushed his tongue along her lower lip. She let out a sweet gasp, her breath a warm sigh against his lips. And then she opened her mouth, her tongue peeking out to say hello.

Tristan tipped his head, deepening the kiss, lightly thrusting his tongue into her mouth to see what she would do. The tip of her tongue swirled around his, a heady dance that turned his stomach into a rollercoaster ride. It dipped and spun as he sucked in a breath, opening his mouth fully and drawing her in.

Her tentative tongue darted out to explore, meeting him halfway before skipping out again. He lightly sucked her bottom lip before she pulled away from him, that sweet sigh tickling the air once more.

Her eyes were wide, her breathing a rapid caper. Tristan lightly squeezed the side of her neck, his thumb resting on the tip of her chin. She was still clutching his shirt, and her mouth opened and closed a couple of times before she finally smiled.

"That was..." She blinked, then swallowed. "That was..."

Tristan grinned. Since when was Helena Thompson ever lost for words?

"Do you want to do it again?"

She bobbed her head and lurched back into his arms, her mouth hitting his with energetic confidence. He held her close, sliding his arms down her back so he could pull her against him. Her slender body fit perfectly within his arms, her inquisitive tongue dancing with his in an all-consuming moment that blocked out the entire world.

Even the creak on the stairs.

22

The Dragon

Helena's tongue was spellbinding. Tristan lost the ability to think clearly. Time stood still; the air was sucked from the room and a soft hum buzzed around him.

And then the attic door rattled.

"Helena, I—"

Her mother's sharp cry ripped the couple apart.

Helena spun, her long braid hitting Tristan's arm. He rested his hand lightly on her hip, supporting her weight when she nearly stumbled.

The dragon's eyes darted to his hand before flaming

with pale blue fire.

"Mother. Wha—I..." Helena's breathing was rapid, not the sweet caper from before but panic-filled puffs that Tristan had never heard before.

Everything about her mother's expression was sharp, from the dip between her eyebrows to the point of her chin. She had the same build and complexion as Helena, a blonde, pale angel, although this one rode a horse of fire and wanted to slash him in half with a blazing sword.

"Get your hands off my daughter." Her voice rang with a low, hard edge, making her sound like a man.

It was damn intimidating.

"Sorry, ma'am. I..." He backed away from Helena, stepping around the quivering girl and thrusting out his hand. "I'm Tristan Parker. I—"

"Get out of my house." The blue fire in her eyes was becoming dark with fury, her molten words hot in the air.

"Mother, please." Helena touched her stomach, leaning forward as she implored, "He's my friend."

The dragon's head snapped towards her, indignant puffs spurting out of her flaring nostrils. "How did he even get in here?"

"He..." Helena pointed over her shoulder at the open window.

"Are you out of your mind?" She stormed across the room, practically knocking Tristan over in her attempt to get to the window.

The pane slammed into place, making Tristan flinch. The woman spun back and snatched Helena's arm, dragging her closer. "You don't even know this boy. How could you be so stupid?"

"He's a good person. He's not going to hurt me." Helena kept her voice even and sweet. Her milky white fingers rested on her mother's cheek. "It's okay. I'm safe. We're safe."

"He is not safe. I don't know him and I want him out of this house!" She accompanied her shout with the point of a shaking finger, snapping her gaze to Tristan. "Get out! Get! Out!"

Tristan shuffled backwards and bumped into the doorframe.

"Mother, please." Helena grasped the dragon's arm, trying to stop her from going after Tristan.

She strained against her daughter and bellowed, "Leave!"

Helena lost the battle, her fingers slipping through the fabric of her mother's blouse as the woman wrenched her arm free.

Tristan's heart raced so hard and fast, he almost felt sick. His gaze shifted to Helena, who gave him a sad, desperate appeal. Her eyes shimmered with tears. The thought of leaving her with her psycho mother nearly killed him.

He stood tall and tried for another attempt at diplomacy.

"Please, ma'am, I don't—"

The dragon's steps were gunshots on the wood. "I will call the police. You're trespassing. You were not invited into this house."

"I invited him." Helena's shout was ignored.

"Leave now!"

"Please, Mrs. Thompson, I—"

"Out!" The wild-eyed woman snatched a book off the shelf and hurled it at Tristan. He raised his arm and batted it away, but had no choice but to bolt when she collected an armful and turned them into cannonballs.

Helena screamed, "Mother, no!" as he raced down the stairs, nearly slipping on the narrow wooden steps. They creaked and groaned beneath him, but the sounds were drowned out by the thump of ominous feet crashing behind him. A book crashed into the wall by his head before flopping to the ground and tumbling down the staircase. He jumped over it, nearly tripping on another book that shot past his ankles.

"Mother, please, stop!" Helena cried again.

Tristan lost his footing and stumbled out of the stairwell, landing in the corridor with a thud.

"Get out!" the dragon raged, her voice taking on a feral quality that was terrifying.

He scrambled up, ducking his shoulder to avoid another book, and took off down the next staircase. He scanned the house, searching for a quick exit. It was like running through a museum—shiny wooden floors covered with Persian rugs and antique furniture. Every picture frame was intricately carved, and every bookcase and piece of furniture looked as though it belonged in Cinderella's castle.

Reaching the bottom stair, Tristan stumbled into a formal-looking parlor. A large harp rested next to an old-fashioned piano, a plush velvet footstool beside it. Shelves lined with hard-covered books and porcelain statuettes covered two of the walls, and above the fireplace rested a cased sword with an elaborately carved handle.

Tristan's lips parted in confusion as he took in the out-of-era surroundings. Helena was living in a madhouse.

Helena.

He glanced over his shoulder, hating the idea of leaving her. But he wasn't about to get bashed in the head with a brick of paper either. He had no doubt the crazy woman would call the cops if she felt like it. He had been trespassing, in a sense. He'd climbed in through a window, after all.

Another book sailed past his head and crashed into the wall behind him, marking the floral print wallpaper.

"Mother!" Helena's voice was high and pitchy—a desperate sound that tore at Tristan's insides.

He stopped next to an antique-looking china cabinet and spun around to face the dragon, lifting his hands as two white flags.

"Please, I'm sorry I upset you."

"Leave! Leave!" The woman's face was deranged with fear and rage. Her pasty white chin trembled, her forehead creased into a vicious scowl. Eyes that he assumed were normally bright blue were two swirling dark masses that Tristan couldn't breach. The woman was certifiably insane. He had no chance of winning any kind of battle.

"I'll leave." He backed toward the main entrance. "Please calm down and I'll go. I just need to know that Helena will be safe."

"She's my daughter! I know what is safe for her. Her well-being is my only concern, which is why you must *get out*."

"I'd never do anything to hurt her. You have to believe that."

"OUT!" she screamed, hurling another book. He ducked and the book hit the picture behind him, splintering the glass.

He spun to look at the destruction, taking in the photo of a happy family with carefree smiles on their faces. They were dressed like characters from a fairytale. A handsome king held his queen close while his blonde princess rested her head on his shoulder, her tiara askew and her smile radiant.

"What have you done?" Helena's mother sucked in a horrified gasp, stumbling to the photo and reaching out for it with shaking fingers. Her breaths were rapidly turning into sobs. "You evil, wretched creature!" She turned to Tristan, her words dripping with venom. "You stay away from my daughter. You stay away from this house. You hear me?"

"Mother, please don't say that." Helena had tears running down her face, stark trails of sadness that marred her porcelain complexion.

"You have one minute to get out." The woman's voice was low and husky.

"Please, it doesn't have to be this way." Helena's tears spurred Tristan into one final attempt, but it was pointless.

The woman looked ready to rip his head off. With an

irate huff, she stormed into the parlor and snatched her phone off the coffee table.

She pushed three digits—*beep, beep, beep*—then held the phone to her ear.

Tristan's time was up.

"All right, all right. I'll go." He backed away, clipping his shoulder on the solid doorframe before turning and walking for the door.

Wrestling with the locks, he flung the door back and jumped onto the porch, scuttling down the steps and heading for the gate.

"Tristan!" Helena raced after him.

He spun on the path, ready to leap forward, catch her hand, and make a run for it. But she stumbled on the stairs, a little yelp popping out of her mouth as she rolled to the ground.

"Helena." Tristan sprinted back, crouching down to help her stand. "Are you okay?"

"I'm fine." Her voice was weak and she hissed when she stood, glancing at her grazed elbow.

"Helena!" The woman's voice was near hysterical, desperate fear lacing each syllable as she stood on the porch. Her skin was stark white, her chest heaving. "Please!" she cried. "It's not safe. It's not safe."

Helena's shoulders slumped. Tristan gripped them, forcing her to face him properly.

"You don't have to go."

A deep sadness washed over her expression and she swallowed. "Listen to her, Tristan. I have to go."

She shuffled out of his grasp, resting her hand on the

banister and looking just a touch afraid. Her eyes darted around the unkempt yard and she blinked a few times before spinning and racing up the stairs.

Her mother's arm wrapped around her shoulders and she pulled her inside. The door slammed shut and the bolts clicked—one, two, three.

Tristan stood by the stairs, straining to hear voices, but all he could make out were soft murmurs. Helena wasn't being screamed at. She was safe inside her home once more and no doubt being fussed over by her psychotic mother.

It ripped his heart out to walk away.

Part of him wanted to call the police himself and have Helena rescued. Her mother obviously hadn't gone through with the call.

But he'd seen the flash of fear on Helena's face. He'd seen the inside of her fairytale house. Would she even be able to handle the real world? She'd be crucified at a normal high school, with her fancy way of talking and her theatrical ways.

With a heavy sigh, he shuffled out the thick gate and back to his house, shoving his hands into his pockets and trying not to remember the ecstasy of Helena's kiss and the intoxicating power she had over him. He wasn't welcome back in that home. He wasn't willing to put Helena through that kind of distress again.

So, really, his only choice was to stay away.

23

Not Enough

Tristan couldn't stay away.

He spent the night dreaming about Helena, locked in her tower and guarded by a vicious dragon. He rose at dawn and leaped to his computer, sending her an email to make sure she was all right.

The email went unanswered.

He sent one every day for the rest of the week, but received nothing in return.

By Friday he could no longer cope, so he climbed the tower once more, but the window was locked. He tapped on the glass, searching for Helena. He was close to giving up when she shuffled into the room, her long hair masking her face. She closed the door behind her and he tapped again.

White-blonde hair floated out around her as she spun. Her puffy red eyes rounded, her soft lips parting as she rushed for the window.

"Let me in," he said softly, not wanting to awaken the dragon.

"I can't." Her voice wobbled. "She bolted it shut." Helena ran her hands over the frame. He craned his head and spotted the metal bracket locking the window in place.

"You should go. I don't want her to catch you." Helena's chin bunched and quivered.

Tristan pressed his hand against the glass. With a watery smile, Helena reached for it, pressing her palm against the pane so their fingers were aligned.

"This can't be over. I've emailed you every day. Why won't you reply?"

Her expression crumpled, her lips pressing into a tight line before she sucked in a breath and admitted, "She's blocked my account. She's deleted everything. I can't even access the Internet anymore."

Anger tore through Tristan's center. "She can't do that," he growled.

"She has." Helena's shoulders slumped, her index finger squeaking on the window as she bent it. "The ban may lift eventually, but I was sneaking a boy into the house and she's just trying to protect me. Maybe it's for the best."

"Don't say that," Tristan huffed. "We didn't do anything wrong! It's not fair. She can't just end us like this."

"She can."

"Not if you don't let her." He stared at the glass, trying to catch her eye and make her see the truth, but Helena refused to look at him. Her hair draped over her face as she dipped her head and sniffed.

"You should go, Tristan. I'm okay. I have our memories."

He thumped the window with the side of his fist. "That's not enough."

"It's all we have." She drew her hand away from the glass and gave him one final glance, her green eyes awash with tears. "They'll be enough." She nodded, stepping away from the window.

"No, wait! Helena, please!"

She shook her head, backing towards the door until she walked into it. Her desperate gaze never left his until she'd managed to turn the handle and spin out of the attic.

Tristan's last glimpse of her was her pale golden locks flying behind her as she sped down the stairs.

He had no choice but to climb down the tower and walk home.

Snatching his bag off the back steps, he shouldered the kitchen door open and stepped inside. The sink was piled high with dirty dishes and he could see clothes spewing out of the laundry room door. The faint sound of a ball game was coming from the living room.

Tristan's shoulders drooped, the energy draining out of him completely.

"Hey, buddy." His dad sauntered into the kitchen, an easy smile on his face. "Yankees are up three nothing against the Sox with two innings to go. Looks like we'll cream 'em again." His chuckle was gleeful and irritating.

Pulling open the fridge, he grabbed a beer and popped the top, rubbing his thumb over the condensation with a grin.

"I take it you're going to watch the rest of the game, then?" Tristan rested his butt against the counter and pressed his palms so hard into the ridge that dents started forming in his skin.

His father shot him an incredulous look. "Of course. Want to join me?"

Tristan's eyes narrowed, his lips bunching into a tight line. "I can't. I've got dishes to do and laundry to clean and dinner to cook! It's not like you're going to do it, right?"

Leon lowered his can, looking at his son like he'd just grown two horns. "What's up?"

"Nothing." Tristan flicked his hand in the air and then scratched his forehead with a frown. "I'm just tired," he mumbled, pushing off the counter and storming from the room. Shooting a dark glare at the TV, he raced up the stairs and slammed his bedroom door.

His father didn't follow him. There was no gentle knock or humble words of apology.

The doorbell rang about forty minutes after Tristan

had flopped onto his bed, and then the smell of pepperoni pizza wafted up the stairs. His stomach grumbled, forcing him off the bed. Slumping down the stairs, he flopped onto the couch, snatching a napkin and a large slice.

They ate in silence, not looking at each other. His father's gaze flicked his way a couple of times, but every time Tristan looked up, his father jerked back toward the screen, shuffling in his seat and clearing his throat.

Tristan rolled his eyes, a deep yearning for Helena causing knots in his stomach and a painful bleed in his chest.

24

Dazed and Confused

Every morning before leaving for school, Tristan stood in his driveway and gazed up at the tower. The trees were starting to bloom and soon the tower would be lost to him.

Each day that passed without a touch of Helena's light stole a little something from him. He spent the weekend holed up in his bedroom, staring at paper cranes and resisting the urge to rip them down. He avoided his father as much as he could, studying in the library after school and coming home with takeout. He'd dump it on the coffee table and then retreat to his room, feigning a heavy study load. His father frowned each night this happened but didn't fight him on it, and so Tristan sank further and further into a morose stupor. He even called and canceled with his mother. The idea of putting on a charade for her and Curtis was too much. She tried to argue, but he won with excuses of schoolwork and extra study. His sullen tone may have put her off as well. She was no doubt relieved not to have to deal with him when he was in one of his moods.

The world around him became dull, the conversations in the hallways were white, static noise, and he struggled to focus on anything clearly.

"Tristan. Tristan?" Mikayla tugged on his arm, jerking him out of his daze. "Hi. Where'd you go?"

He shook his head, shrugging with a frown.

"I've been chasing you down two corridors. Thankfully you were walking like a low-battery robot, so you were easy to catch." She grinned, her freckles twitching with the rise of her cheeks. She caught the edge of her lip with her teeth and kind of cringed up at him. "You know you've got English now, right?"

"Yeah, so?"

"So." She looked confused, and then her expression crinkled with worry. "Well, you're heading in the opposite direction. Are you skipping out?"

He closed his eyes and shook his head, pinching the bridge of his nose and turning back the way he'd come.

Mikayla's small hand stopped him, wrapping around his wrist and tugging him still.

"If you need someone to talk to, I could meet you under the bleachers." She grinned. "I kind of owe you one."

"No, I'm good."

She gave his forearm a light squeeze. "You don't look good, Tristan. Whatever's tearing you apart, you either need to do something to stop it...or you need to let it go."

"I know," he murmured. "I...I just don't know how."

Her soft hazel gaze searched his face. "I'm always here to listen, if you need a friend. A burden shared is a burden halved, you know."

His gaze snapped to hers, his eyebrows wrinkling with a fleeting frown. "That's what my friend says."

"Well, he must be a smart guy." She chuckled.

"She," he whispered brokenly.

Mikayla's face puckered with concern and she moved to step in front of him, but he turned out of her way before she could. He was sure she was staring at him as he shuffled off to English, but he couldn't look back to check.

All he wanted was Helena. He couldn't let her go...but he didn't know how to get her back either.

"Right, we're starting a new topic today." Miss Warren clipped through the class, dropping assignment papers on each desk.

Tristan picked his up and grimaced.

Poetry. Aw, crap. How the heck was he supposed to survive that? The only reason he'd done so well on *Romeo and Juliet* was because of Helena. He'd flunk for sure without her guidance.

Despair pierced him as he imagined going home to his morose house and enduring the unit alone. He'd try to decipher the confusing text with no one to help him. His father was useless when it came to homework.

Who was he kidding? His father was useless when it came to everything except drinking beer and watching TV.

Tristan lifted the page and read the assignment. They had to select a poem and analyze it, trying to draw out the writer's meaning between the lines and figure out what kind of lessons the author wanted to teach the reader.

"I call bullshit," Tristan muttered, slapping his paper down.

"Something to share, Mr. Parker?" Miss Warren dropped the leftover papers on her desk and faced him with a smile.

He shook his head, pressing his elbows into the desk and keeping his head down.

"Who's your favorite poet?" Her voice, usually so calming, grated on his nerves.

He gritted his teeth and shrugged. "I'm not really into poetry."

She nodded, a soft smile brushing her lips. "Well, let's hope I can change your mind." Leaning back against her desk, she shook her head to flick the long sideways bangs out of her eyes and asked the whole class. "Anyone else? Who has a favorite poet, or already knows the poem they want to pull apart and analyze?"

Tristan slumped down in his seat and let the answers turn to fuzz. The paper crinkled in his grasp, and it was an effort to even swallow. He was going to fail this assignment…and he didn't even care.

25

Miss Warren's Romantic Heart

The bell rang, freeing Tristan from the torture of poetic prose and brilliant minds that had died decades before.

"Tristan, may I have a word, please?" Miss Warren hindered his retreat. A few students eyed him as they brushed past and out the door. He turned sideways, letting the room clear before shuffling back into it. Miss Warren walked around her desk, smoothing down the back of her beige skirt and taking a seat.

He stood in front of her, his jaw clenched as his gaze

traveled the front panel of her desk.

"What's up?" His teacher rested her chin on her knuckles, settling in for a conversation Tristan didn't really want to have.

He shrugged.

"Tristan Parker, you have a burden weighing you down. I have no idea what it is and it may not be my place to even ask. I'd love to refer you to the school counselor, but I have a sneaking suspicion you'd refuse to go."

He pursed his lips, the sudden silence between them thick and awkward.

Miss Warren huffed out her nose and pulled a sheet of paper from underneath her planner. She slapped it on her desk, giving him a pointed look.

Tristan leaned forward to glimpse his Shakespeare test. A vivid F was circled in the top right corner.

"Explain to me how you can get an A+ in your assignment work and an F on the final test. Where were you last Monday?"

Tristan frowned and mumbled, "I was here."

"Your body may have been here, but your mind certainly wasn't." Her eyebrows lifted, her stern expression giving him no comfort. "Do you have to catch the bus after school?"

"No, I've got my bike."

"Good, then sit." She pointed at a front row chair.

With a heavy sigh, Tristan slipped the bag off his shoulder and slumped into the desk.

"You know this'll go much faster if you lose the

scowl." Miss Warren's right eyebrow peaked as she dipped her head with a pointed warning.

His jaw worked to the side and he looked away from her, training his eyes on the door he desperately wanted to escape through.

"Now, I am willing to let you redo this test, claiming that sickness hindered you from success when you first did it. But before I offer that, I need to know if it's worth the effort I will have to go through."

His lips pulled into a straight line and after a long, slow beat he shook his head. "I can't pass it."

"Why?" She leaned forward, her gaze shifting to one of such sincere concern that Tristan felt his insides begin to fracture.

"I..." He swallowed, picking at the desktop and struggling to breathe past the rock in his throat.

"The girl who helped you with *Romeo and Juliet*. Is she still around?"

He nodded, then shook his head, his chin trembling.

"What happened?" His teacher's voice dropped to a husky caress that yanked the truth right out of him.

"Her mother." His laugh was dry and brittle. "She doesn't want me to see her anymore. She's kind of paranoid. She caught me over there and won't let me back in. The woman's psycho."

"Is this friend of yours safe?" Miss Warren threaded her fingers together, an uneasy frown flashing over her expression.

Tristan didn't know how to respond. If he said no, Miss Warren was the kind of teacher to take that stuff seriously. She'd be calling child services before he even left the school grounds. That could save Helena. She could go into foster care... She could...

Foster care?

Who the hell are you kidding?

Leaving that safe haven of hers would kill her. As much as he wanted to set her free, he didn't want her drowning either.

Pressing his lips together, he forced a nod. "Yeah. Her mother loves her. They have a good relationship, I think."

"So, maybe not so much psycho as overprotective?" Miss Warren's elegant finger brushed beneath her chin, the silver ring on her middle finger catching Tristan's eye. He stared at the intricate oval design. It reminded him of the vines wrapped around Helena's tower.

"Yeah, you could say that," he mumbled.

"I take it she doesn't want some strange boy stealing her precious daughter away." Miss Warren winked.

Tristan's chuckle was hollow and raspy. "I'd never steal her. I just want to be with her. I miss her."

Miss Warren's gaze softened, her lips rising with sweet affection. She was no doubt swooning at the idea of young love.

Tristan blushed and looked back to the desktop.

"Young love has to be one of the most powerful forces on this planet." Miss Warren chuckled. "Throw a little forbidden in there too and you've got something quite intoxicating."

"Not being allowed to see her isn't why I want her so much."

Miss Warren tipped her head at Tristan's desperate whisper. "Then why do you want her?"

"Because..." He raised his hand, then squeezed the back of his neck with a sigh. "She makes me feel happy and like I'm a good version of myself when I'm with her. She sees me, you know? I could tell her anything. I love that we can just sit and shoot the breeze for a whole afternoon and it's like no time has passed. She inspires me and feels perfect in my arms—her sweet scent and candy lips..." His voice died off with a floaty whisper. The dreamy smile on Tristan's lips lingered for a moment, until he caught Miss Warren's delighted expression.

Jerking in his seat, he sat up and cleared his throat, his cheeks firing red. Miss Warren laughed softly, spinning the ring on her finger while he ducked his head and scratched the nonexistent itch between his eyebrows.

"You've got it pretty bad, I see."

He shrugged.

"I can understand why this is tearing you apart."

His lips pursed and he shook his head, his shoulders hitching again.

Miss Warren cleared her throat, the chair scraping on the floor as she stood. Her shoes clicked on the shiny surface as she walked around and took a seat at the desk beside him. "You know, Romeo and Juliet broke the rules to be together."

Tristan scoffed. "And look what happened to them."

"But look what they had before it fell apart." Miss Warren smiled and then sighed. "I'm not trying to encourage you to break the rules and upset her mother, but sometimes we have to snatch whatever moments of happiness we can." She rested her long fingers on her upper chest and gave it a little tap. "Just imagine if Juliet had locked herself away and ignored Romeo. She would have missed out on this pure, magical moment in her life—a sheer taste of happiness that was so compelling she just *had* to follow her heart."

Tristan scratched his eyebrow, his lips dipping. "Sometimes I wonder if it's best to not know what you're missing."

Miss Warren's head tipped to the side, her fine sandy locks resting on her shoulder. "Do you really want to live your life that way, Tristan? Shuffling through it with blinders on, ignoring everything it has to offer?"

He shrugged, his lips pursing as he shook his head.

"Okay, let me put it this way." She tapped her finger on the desk. "You are currently miserable and you need to do something to snap out of this stupor. If being with this girl makes you happy, which we both know it does, then you need to find a way to make that happen. Life is too short to waste on wishing. Sometimes you have to chase after what you want."

He gave her a skeptical frown. "Even if it gets me in trouble?"

Miss Warren's lips twitched. "Some things on this earth are worth fighting for, and I believe love is one of them. You're not breaking any laws by pursuing this girl, are you?"

"Not unless her mother tries to get a restraining order against me."

"Well, until she does, I suggest you make the most of it." Miss Warren winked. "Be brave, Tristan. Go get your girl." She nodded her chin towards the door. "And I'll arrange for you to retake that test next week."

With a slightly confused frown, he rose from his seat, shuffling out the door with a bemused grin.

Did that just happen?

He shook his head with a chuckle, his sneakers squeaking on the shiny floor as he made his way out past the last few stragglers and down the front steps of his school.

26

An Alternate Reality

Tristan was still tripping over his little chat with Miss Warren as he parked his bike in the garage. He didn't know how he was supposed to see Helena again. Yeah, he could climb the tower, but with the windows bolted and the dragon on duty it'd be pretty damn hard.

He wasn't sure if he was up for the fight either.

Avoiding drama and conflict was his MO. He wasn't too keen on running headfirst into battle with a psycho, book-throwing dragon.

He grabbed the two bags of groceries he'd collected on

the way home and then headed up the back steps. Flicking the door open, he walked into the kitchen and stopped, his eyes bugging out at the sight of his father standing by the sink, a dishtowel slung over his shoulder as he rinsed off a plate. A pot was bubbling on the stovetop, a box of Kraft Mac n' Cheese sitting next to it.

"Uh, what are you doing?" Tristan placed the groceries down and slid the bag off his shoulder. It thudded to the floor.

His father gave him a lopsided grin. "I figured it was about time I gave cooking a try."

Tristan's forehead crinkled and he looked over his shoulder, wondering when he'd accidentally walked into an alternate universe.

"I don't understand what's happening right now. Why aren't you on the couch drinking beer?"

His father lowered the dish scrubber with a heavy sigh, his head drooping between his broad shoulders.

"Tristan..." He sighed again, resting his dripping hands against the side of the sink. "What you said a few days ago really got to me. I know I'm a slow, lumbering dinosaur when it comes to dealing with emotions. The divorce, it...it really shut me down. I guess I forgot to notice how much it affected you too." He spun to face his son, snatching the towel off his shoulder and drying his hands. "I can't tell you how glad I am that you chose to stay with me, but it always felt like a weird decision. I didn't know how to help you. I didn't know what to say or do to make you happy. But then you kind of picked up on your own. You started smiling again and..." His father's lips lifted at the edges. "I started to feel like we could do this, you know?" His face bunched with a quick frown. "But the last week or so it's just gone. You're back to living like a zombie, and I...I don't know if I can cope with that."

He kept his eyes on his fingers, drying them until the skin was tinged pink. "Now that I've seen you happy, seeing you miserable again is killing me." He waved his hand in the air and then pointed to the stovetop. The lid on the pot jumped and rattled. Leon lurched toward it, lifting the lid and giving it a quick stir with the wooden spoon. He glanced over his shoulder with a sheepish grin. "I thought maybe I should step up and start playing Dad for a change. Sixteen-year-old high school kids should not be cooking dinner every night."

Tristan flashed him a sad smile, a thick lump forming in his throat. He nodded a couple of times and finally croaked, "Thanks, Dad."

His father brushed the air with a bashful smile. "Why don't you get cleaned up? Dinner will be ready soon."

Still in a mild state of shock, Tristan did as he was told without argument, clomping up the stairs and reeling over the total weirdness of his day.

Scrubbing a hand over his face, he dumped his bag and kicked off his shoes, heading back down to the kitchen to see if he could help.

His father wouldn't let him do a thing except unpack the groceries, and twenty minutes later they were sitting down to a slightly crispy version of Mac n' Cheese and a salad that looked like it'd been made by a five-year-old wielding a machete.

His father shoved a forkful of food in his mouth and wrestled with a grimace, eventually throwing his son a tight smile. Tristan fought the urge to laugh and shuffled in his seat, scooping up a small forkful and tasting it.

He swallowed down the ashy food and cleared his throat. "Ketchup?"

"Good idea."

Tristan jumped up and grabbed the bottle from the fridge, handing it to his father with a light snicker.

"I'll get better," he mumbled.

"Thanks for trying." Tristan smiled—a small, closed-mouth one, but genuine.

His dad squirted a blob of ketchup onto his plate and handed it to his son. "So, ah, what, um, seems to be bothering you this week?"

"Dad, really?" Tristan tipped his head with a pitiful frown, snapping the ketchup bottle closed and placing it down between them.

"Come on, buddy, I used to be a good dad. We used to go out back and chuck a ball around. You'd tell me everything."

Tristan swirled his fork through his ketchup. "I'm not a kid anymore."

His father nodded. "Yeah, I know it, but you can still tell me anything."

What was it with people and trying to get him to talk? The day had been stuffed full of them. Tristan slumped back in his seat and started spinning his water glass around.

"Is it about a girl?" His dad took another bite of his food, his Adam's apple jerking as he swallowed it down.

Tristan's gaze shot to his father's before it dashed back to the glass in his hands.

Out of the corner of his eye, he saw his father nod. "She's pretty awesome, huh?"

Tristan's lips rose before he could stop them.

His father chuckled, grabbing his glass of water and taking a quick sip before running his tongue along his bottom teeth. "What's her name?"

"Helena," Tristan whispered.

"Nice." His dad nodded again. "You know the first girl I ever fell for, I said her name that way too."

Tristan's eyebrows bunched and he glanced at his dad. "What way?"

"Aw, you know, whispering it like that...as if the word tasted like cotton candy in my mouth."

Tristan grinned, his cheeks starting to burn with color. His father gave him a light punch on the arm.

"Son, you got it bad." He chuckled and shot him a sympathetic half-smile. "She didn't dump you, did she?"

"Things got complicated." Tristan tipped his head.

"You think you can work it out?" The fork scraped his father's plate as he scooped up more food.

Tristan picked at his salad, flicking a large hunk of carrot to the side. "I'd like to. I just don't know if I should."

His father tapped his fork on the plate. "I once dated a girl whose father hated me. I don't know why. He was the kind of man to greet you at the door with a twelve-gauge shotgun in his hands."

Tristan's eye bulged.

"But I liked her too much to not at least try. So one night, after dark, I snuck over there and threw stones at her window. She opened it up, her smile radiant, her pale white hair glistening in the moonlight..."

"Dad." Tristan snapped his fingers, trying to bring his father back to earth.

The large man shook his head, his lips curling with a sheepish grin. "Her name was Mandy, and I was a lovesick fifteen-year-old."

"What happened?"

"We snuck out that night. I took her to a fair just outside of town and we had the time of our lives. I won her a panda bear in one of those shooting games and we shared cotton candy and kissed behind the fortune teller's booth."

Tristan chuckled. "Did you get in trouble?"

"Oh yeah, I thought he was going to blow my head off when I walked her back home. She was grounded for a month and I was banned from walking anywhere near the house. My father chewed me out and told me to stay away from her."

Shuffling in his seat, Tristan rested his arms against the table. "Did you?"

"We tried pursuing it for a while, but it got too hard and complicated. She moved out of town at the end of the year, so it was over. It was worth it though, even for just that one night...a treasured memory."

"A paper crane," Tristan murmured to himself.

27

Helena's Fairytale

"Rapunzel!" Tristan tried to shout and whisper at the same time so as not to get caught. His voice was going hoarse with the effort.

Flinging another pebble at the window, he bit the inside of his cheek, hoping he was aiming for the right one. As soon as night had fallen, he'd snuck next door—crept through the bush like a commando warrior and scouted out the house. The tower window wasn't an option, so he had to find her bedroom. He didn't know the house well, but Helena had mentioned that her room was *beneath them*. They'd been sitting on the sofa at the time, so Tristan snuck around the other side of the house, lined up with what he hoped was her bedroom window, and started throwing pebbles.

"Rapunzel!" he whisper-barked again.

One more stone throw and a dim light flicked on. It must have been a lamp because the glow was soft, only growing slightly when the curtain parted.

Helena's pretty face popped into view. Tristan could hardly see her, but he was sure her lips parted with surprise before she unlatched the window and threw it open.

Her voice was high with surprise. "Tristan? What are you doing here?"

"Rapunzel." He spread his arms wide. "Let down your hair."

She giggled, covering her mouth with her hand before flashing him a desperate look of worry.

"Please," he whispered. "I have to see you again."

Her expression melted to a swoon that had her biting her lower lip and disappearing inside. Tristan bounced from one foot to the next, chewing his cheek raw as he kept an eye out for the dragon.

What felt like an eternity later, two white sheets that had been tied together were thrown from the window. Tristan jumped up and grabbed the rope, grunting as he pulled himself up. He reached the lip of the slanted roof and scrambled to Helena's window.

Clutching the edge of the sill, he leaned his head inside. His face was captured by her long, soft fingers, and before he could even speak her lips were on his. They were supple and warm, and he melted against them, breathing in her scent and floating out of time for a moment.

She pulled back and pressed her forehead against his. "You shouldn't be here."

"I can't stay away. You have to let me in."

She stole a look over her shoulder, eyeing the bedroom door. "You know I can't. It's too risky."

He cupped her cheek, caressing her delicate jaw with his thumb. "Then come with me."

"Run away?" She tried to step out of his grasp, but he caught the back of her neck and held her steady.

"Just for tonight." He grinned. "One date. Please, let me show you."

Her forehead crinkled and she brushed her fingers down his cheek.

"I'll have you home by midnight, I promise." He winked, making her lips twitch with a grin.

"Mother *is* already in bed. She's taken her sleeping herbs too, so I guess it would be safe enough, but..." Her face bunched with indecision.

"I just want to give you a few more paper cranes, that's all. One night, Helena. Please."

That did it. The paper cranes thing. She was all over that.

Her eyes began to dance, her lips rising into a radiant grin.

"Let me get dressed." She spun away and Tristan dipped back down onto the roof to give her some privacy.

More and more stars were littering the sky as night set in. Tristan grinned, gazing up at the brilliant landscape, grateful for the crystal-clear night. The air was definitely getting warm, that harsh winter chill being replaced with a fresh spring breeze. Blossoms were budding on trees and the hope of summer flittered through the air.

Tristan smiled. He wanted everything about the date to be perfect. There was a chance this was the only one she'd ever get. He had to make it count.

"I'm ready." She appeared behind the curtain again, looking exquisite in a pale pink dress that hugged the curves of her torso before floating down to her knees.

"You look like a princess." He grinned.

"Well, you did call me Rapunzel." She brushed a long lock of hair over her shoulder and gave him a shy smile.

"Come on." He shimmied to the side and held out his hand, helping her through the wooden frame. Her ballet slippers skidded on the slates. She yelped and flailed.

Tristan reached for her, catching her against his side and holding her close. "It's okay, I've got you. Climb on my back."

Her arms were taut wire as she did so, her legs wrapping around his hips. Her breath teased his neck as she clung to him, making Tristan smile.

Not wanting to scare her, he took his time, gently descending the roof and slipping down the side of the house. He let go of the sheet and landed with a light thud. Helena's arms tensed around his throat but then loosened as she slid off his back.

She looked around her, fear and wonder playing over

her features. "I haven't been outside like this for six years. I've grown so much in that time, you'd think the world would seem a little smaller." She looked up at the sky, a soft breath whistling out of her. "But it's so big."

Tristan took her hand, threading his fingers through hers. "It's going to be okay. I'll keep you safe."

Her head bobbed like a jackknife but she smiled, squeezing his hand and letting him lead her off the property.

They eased out the gate, wincing at its soft creak, then hit the sidewalk and headed down the road. Tristan wanted to take her into town. Church Street Marketplace was always so magical at night and Friday was open with market stalls and that happy end-of-the-week buzz that seemed contagious. Helena would love it.

Her fingers remained tightly clasped within his, her muscles growing more taut with each step down the darkened streets. Squeezing her digits, he swung their arms and tried to distract her with talk of something she'd love.

"So, we've started a poetry unit a school."

Her gaze snapped his way. "Oh, how wonderful."

"Yeah." Tristan's chuckle was terse and sarcastic.

Helena ignored his derogatory tone and smiled. "Do you have an assignment?"

Tristan nodded. "We have to analyze a poem."

Her hand captured his arm, squeezing his elbow tightly. "What are you going to pick?" Distracted by the literary adventure, Helena's eyes began to dance, her tight fear making room for her passion.

"I was going to ask you."

"Hmmm." She looked to the sky, her cheeks puffing out while she thought. She studied the wondrous expanse above them, the twinkling diamonds in the night and whispered, *"The wind was a torrent of darkness among the gusty trees. The moon was a ghostly galleon tossed upon cloudy seas. The road was a ribbon of moonlight over the purple moor, and the highwayman came riding–riding–riding–The highwayman came riding, up to the old inn-door."*

The magical way she said the lines stirred Tristan's heart. He gazed down at her, studying every inch of her perfect face. "That sounds awesome. What poem is that?"

"'The Highway Man' by Alfred Noyes." She smiled. "You must choose it. It's a tragic, beautiful tale of love, passion, and chivalry."

Tristan's eyes narrowed. "There's death in it, isn't there?"

Helena giggled at his sardonic tone, resting her cheek against his shoulder. "Tragedies make the most compelling stories, Tristan, really they do."

He shook his head with a snicker. "I'll think about it."

"I wish I could help you with the assignment," she whispered.

"We could rewrite the ending," he murmured.

Helena's cheek rose on his shoulder. He didn't have to see her smile to feel the warmth of it.

"I've missed you." He brushed his lips against her forehead. "How've you been?"

She rubbed her thumb over the back of his hand as they turned the corner, nearing the middle of town.

"Lonely. My stories and imagination were always enough...until I met you."

He nudged her lightly with his shoulder. "I'm not going anywhere, Helena. I can still be here for you, if you let me."

They came to a busier road and paused to let the traffic pass. Helena's nostrils flared, her wide eyes drinking in the zip of cars and flickering streetlights. "Let's see if we survive this night first, shall we?"

He chuckled, pulling their hands to his lips and kissing her knuckles. She rested her head against his shoulder once more, but the second they turned the corner and hit Church Street Marketplace, her head popped up with a delighted laugh.

"Oh, Tristan. It's beautiful."

The radiant wonder on her face made Tristan glow. He couldn't take his eyes off her face as she drank in the delight of the quaint walking street. Tress lined the cobbled walkway, dressed up with golden, glowing fairy lights. People milled around the market stalls, eating mouth-watering goodies and sipping on hot apple cider. The smell of fresh baking and cinnamon floated in the air around them.

A group of young women passed by, talking a mile a minute and swooning over a necklace that one of them had just purchased. Helena jumped out of the way, snuggling against Tristan. He let go of her hand and wrapped his arm around her shoulders.

"If it's too much, we can find somewhere quieter."

"No." She shook her head. "I want to see."

He squeezed her against him and led her through the throng. Her arm wrapped around his waist and she curled her fingers into his sweater. He was her protector for the night and he wouldn't have it any other way. They ambled along in no particular hurry. The first thing Tristan bought her was a hot cocoa, creamy and peppered with mini marshmallows. The moans of pleasure she made while drinking it were enough for him to offer to buy her another one, but she refused, instead drawn towards a stall of handmade jewelry.

The little table was covered with necklaces and bracelets, and the beads were colorful and unique—all different shapes, sizes, and combinations. Helena touched the exquisite creations.

"These are amazing." She lifted a necklace, marveling at the shiny beads. "You made these yourself?"

The shop owner—an older lady with wrinkled skin and wild hair held off her face with a long scarf—nodded with a grin. "Yes."

"Such talent."

The shop owner blushed. "Thank you."

"A master craftswoman." Helena grinned. "This jewelry is fit for a queen."

The shop owner chuckled, her shoulders rising in a bashful shrug.

Tristan couldn't help marveling at Helena's beautiful spirit. She'd been trapped in a tower for six years and the second she was set free she was able to spread her sunshine like a sweet fragrance. It was a sin that her mother kept her locked away. The world deserved

Helena's light.

A dark rage spiked through Tristan as he thought of the unfairness of it all, but it was tempered by Helena's sweet laughter.

Running his hand up her back, he lightly kneaded her neck and whispered into her ear, "Choose one."

She turned to him, catching her breath and automatically shaking her head. "I couldn't possibly."

"Please." Tristan touched his nose to her cheek. "I want you to have one, to remember this night."

Her lips rose with a smile. "I can assure you, nothing will make me forget this night."

"Still. I want you to have something."

Pressing her lips together, she looked back at the stall, eyeing the merchandise with longing before turning back to him. "Are you sure?"

"Of course." Tristan pulled out his wallet. "Choose what you like."

Tristan wondered if she'd ever had a Christmas the way she was looking at the stall and hesitating over buying such a small trinket. Her fingers ran over the different necklaces, finally pausing on a brown leather band that held an oval. Painted on the golden-colored disk was the silhouette of a bird flying free.

"That's it," Tristan whispered. "That's the one you should have." He brushed her hair over her shoulder, leaning his chin in its place and sliding his arm around her waist. "It's perfect for you."

She clutched it in her hand and nodded. Tristan paid the stall owner and helped Helena put the necklace on. It hung just above her perfect breasts. She ran her fingers down the leather and pressed the disk against her skin.

"I love it. Thank you." Placing a sweet kiss on his lips, she wrapped her arms around him and he lifted her off the ground, spinning her gently before placing her back down and walking on.

He kept his arm around her waist as much as he could, delighting in her laughter, her wonder and the brightness of her smile.

28

A Thousand Cranes

The lake water lapped against the edge of the pier, creating the perfect soundtrack. The temperature had dropped, the air now a crisp companion. Tristan slid off his jacket and wrapped it around Helena's shoulders.

She grinned at him, pressing her arm against his side and nestling her head on his shoulder.

"Thank you for this evening," she whispered. "It has been perfect."

He smiled and skimmed his lips against her cool forehead.

"I want to give you more." He kicked his feet in the air, crossing his ankles and letting them swing out over the water.

Helena's only response was a soft sigh.

Tristan didn't know how to reply. Instead he silently sat on the pier, fighting the urge to rant at her mother's narrow-minded unfairness.

As if reading his mind, Helena murmured, "She was such a different person before my father died." She adjusted her head on his shoulder.

"What was she like?"

"Music. She was like a cheerful polka on a sunny day, and then when it rained she was a melancholy concerto. When she was angry, she was a symphony."

Tristan smiled, resisting the urge to mutter, *I know.*

"Everything about her was glorious and whimsical. Her laughter was so melodic and carefree. Papa brought out the beauty in her. He'd watch her like she was the most unique, stunning creature on the earth. The love they had for each other was like nothing I've ever seen...and the day he died, it all ended. She died with him and someone else possessed her body, a fear-filled woman who was lost." Helena's voice dropped to a whisper. "I didn't know what to do. I was fighting my own despair and it just seemed easier to let her be what she needed to be. I ran away and hid inside my imagination, in books and stories that always had a triumphant ending, and the ones that didn't, I'd rewrite them. It got me through."

"But is it enough?" He lifted his shoulder, forcing her

to sit up and look at him. "Can it get you through the rest of your life?"

"I'm not sure anymore." Her voice caught, the wind catching her hair and playfully teasing it.

Tristan reached for her hand, pressing it against his chest. "Are you afraid your mother will never get better? That you'll be trapped looking after her for the rest of your life?"

"Yes and no, I suppose." She sighed. "Caring for someone who needs me is a good thing. If I die tomorrow, I know I'll have done what was right. Papa would be proud of me and I could never regret that. I just—" Her breath caught, cutting off her words.

"You just what?" Tristan searched her face.

She sniffed. "Sometimes I fear that I'm going to disappear. That life will pass by and I'll have nothing to show for it. I'll leave no footprint behind me. I've spent so much of my life shut away. Some days it feels like I don't exist."

"You'll always exist." Tristan squeezed her hand, tapping it against his chest. "No matter what happens to you…or me. You will *always* exist in my life." He lifted her fingers and pressed them against his lips. "We have to find a way to be together."

"I don't want to burden your life with my choice. You must go and live it." A tear trickled down the edge of her nose and Tristan wiped it away before it could reach her trembling lips.

"How can I ever live it when I know you're trapped? I want you to be happy."

"I am."

"Not completely." Tristan shook his head, the water surging near his feet as if feeling his emotion. "You deserve everything, Helena. You deserve the world."

"She's so afraid, Tristan. How can I leave her?" Her face crumpled and she looked out across the water, the dark expanse making her shrink back against him.

"You need to get her help. There are professionals who can walk her through this. It doesn't have to stay this way."

"You can't help someone who doesn't want to know. She won't listen."

Tristan huffed and turned away to stare at the dark lake.

She reached for his face, her fingers feather-light as they caressed his rigid jaw. "Let's not ruin this magical moment."

Softened by her words, Tristan curled his fingers around the back of her neck and kissed her forehead. He closed his eyes and breathed in her jasmine scent. "No matter what happens or how long it takes, I promise...we'll always be together."

She closed her eyes and smiled, one final tear rolling down the edge of her face. She brushed it away with a small chuckle and opened her eyes. Her green gaze hit him in the chest, making his heart beat hard and fast.

"You've given me a thousand hanging cranes tonight, but that is the best one of all."

He grinned, leaning forward and lightly placing his lips on hers. She sighed against him, a sweet sound that had him pulling her onto his lap. Her dress draped over his knees, her slender body pressing against him. Running his hands around her waist, he trailed them beneath his jacket and up her back.

Her lips parted, her teasing tongue darting into his mouth. He responded with a sigh of his own, pressing his fingers into her back and drawing her close.

The night air kissed their skin, the faint breeze rustling Helena's hair as the world around them disappeared. All that existed were lips, dancing tongues, and the racing hearts of two young lovers.

Lightly sucking her bottom lip, Tristan pulled back enough to gaze into her eyes.

"I—I love you, Helena."

Her eyes sparkled, her lips rising into a magical grin. "You've owned my heart since the day you climbed in my window, Tristan Alex Parker. I shall love you for all eternity."

Their lips met again for an exquisite kiss. Heat and light swirled into an intoxicating dance that Tristan would feel for the rest of his life.

29

Pure Magic

They walked home hand in hand, their fingers threaded together in an unbreakable bond. Tristan squeezed her fingers and grinned yet again. There was no such thing as walking when he was beside her, just floating in the air.

Helena's sweet smile made his heart trip and stumble, and the memory of her lips caressing his was enough to keep him awake for hours. He didn't want the night to end and she mustn't have either, because the closer they reached to home, the slower their steps became.

She rested her head on his shoulder while they ambled in the quiet darkness. Her long, delicate fingers played with the necklace he'd bought her. He kissed the top of her head, feeling like a king.

As if reading his mind, Helena began to hum "Lavenders Blue Dilly Dilly."

He remembered his mother dancing around the house to the same tune, an entranced smile on her lips as she waltzed with the air.

"When I am king, dilly dilly, you shall be queen," Tristan softly sang.

Helena giggled. "I never thought I could get you singing. I really have triumphed."

He grinned, glad the darkness could hide his blazing cheeks. Looking across the street, he gazed at the patch of grass where it had all started.

If those kids hadn't been playing ball...if they hadn't hit one into his driveway...if the baseball hadn't been so precious...

He never would have met her.

Pulling in a grateful breath, Tristan tried to ward off the weight of their impending goodbye.

Creeping through the thick grass, Tristan led her to the hanging sheet. It still floated in the breeze against the house, undiscovered. They stood beneath it, gazing at each other in the moonlight.

The sadness in Helena's smile tore at Tristan's heart. He didn't want to return her. He wanted to keep her by his side...forever. But that was her choice, and he could tell by her lack of words that she had made her decision.

She wouldn't leave her mother, not even for him.

"Come on." Tristan spun around and crouched so she could climb onto his back. Her arms and legs snaked around him. She locked her ankles at his waist and he gripped the rope. It took all his strength to haul them both up. It was lucky she was a lightweight.

With a grunt, he slapped his hand on the roof and dug his fingers into the slates. As soon as Helena could reach, she climbed off his back and scrambled up to the window. He stayed close behind her, making sure she didn't slip and fall.

Holding her hips, he balanced her so she could climb through the window and then followed her through. He couldn't linger—it was too risky. He didn't want her getting in trouble.

Helena slid his jacket off and handed it back to him. He gripped it in his fist with a heavy sigh before pulling it on.

"Thank you for a...magical...date." Helena's smile lacked its usual luster.

He collected her hand, pressing his lips against her knuckles. "It was my pleasure, believe me."

Her cheeks bloomed with a cherry sweetness and she dipped her head. Long hair cascaded over her shoulders, hiding her face from him.

He wasn't sure what to say, so he dropped her hand and forced himself back to the window.

"Wait." Her gasp was soft and caught in her throat.

Pivoting on his heel, he spun back in time to catch her against him. He drew her close, breathing in her jasmine and running his hand down her back until they were fused together.

"You'll return, won't you?" Her whisper was frantic.

"Of course," he murmured into her hair before pulling back to look at her. Running his finger down her hairline, he tucked a lock of hair behind her ear. "But only if you want me to."

"I do." She clutched his wrist, tears glistening in her eyes.

"Hey, what is it?"

She swallowed and blinked, the light breeze coming through the window making goose bumps ripple over her skin. "I was scared tonight, but I wanted to be with you, so I ignored my fear...and...and I had the most amazing night of my life. I've never felt so alive." She gazed into his eyes, brushing her fingers down his cheek. "And now that you're leaving I realize..." Her breath caught and she had to swallow before she could go on. "I can't bear the thought of never seeing you again. I need more, Tristan. I want you to take me out on a hundred dates. A thousand."

"I'll take you on a million," he whispered, resting his forehead against hers. "You don't have to stay trapped here forever. We can get your mom help. We can get you out of this."

She nodded, sniffing at her tears and giving him a watery smile.

"Is that what you want?"

She nodded again. "I *need* to be with you. I want to live in this world. I want to leave a footprint. I want...a life outside of these walls."

Her words set his heart alight. With a soft smile, he reached for her lips, his body trembling with excitement. Their tongues danced for a moment, tying their fates together.

Pulling back, Tristan held her neck, rubbing his thumb across her cheek and smiling down at her. "We'll make it happen, Helena. I promise you, I'll get you out of here."

The spark was back in her eyes, the vow of freedom giving her a radiant glow.

A creak sounded above them. Whether it was the wind or a dragon, they weren't sure, but it was enough to pull them apart. Tristan snuck to the window, the idea of leaving no longer so painful.

Easing into the darkness, he steadied himself on the slates, clutching the sheet rope and easing down the roof.

"I'll see you soon," Helena whispered into the darkness. Her pale hand reached for his. He leaned back so they could touch one last time.

"It's a promise." He kissed her knuckles and left before he was tempted to climb back through the window.

He landed in the grass with a faint thump, wiping his hands on his butt as the sheet was pulled away from him. He grinned up at the night sky, feeling lighter than air.

Practically prancing home, he waltzed in the back door and practically jumped out of his skin when he spotted his father in the doorway.

"Whoa!" He clutched his chest and leaned forward

with a gasp.

A stifled laugh eased out of his father as he lumbered into the kitchen. "Where've you been?"

Tristan looked up and shook his head. "Just out." It was impossible to hide his smile. His lips rose of their own accord, pulling his face into a dopey grin.

His father snickered. "Right. *Just* out."

"Yep." Tristan nodded, biting his lips together. It didn't work; his smile fought against him and spread his cheeks wide.

Clearing his throat, his father ambled to the fridge, patting his son's shoulder as he brushed past. "Helena. That's her name, right?"

Tristan nodded.

His father gave him a knowing wink, shaking his head with a look that Tristan swore was pride.

"Well, I'm gonna head to bed. Get some sleep." Tristan pointed over his shoulder.

"Good luck with that." His dad pulled out a Dr. Pepper, opening the can with a wink.

Tristan walked out of the room, still grinning as he headed up the stairs. He didn't know how he was going to get Helena out of that house, but he'd find a way to keep his promise.

Part of him was tempted to pull out his laptop and start researching everything he could on people with phobias, where they could get help, how to involve child services, but the idea tasted sour in this mouth.

No, he wanted to savor the night. So instead, he reached for a paper crane and a pen.

First date with Helena—pure magic.

Grabbing the nylon string she'd given him, he cut a longer piece than normal, tied a knot and threaded the bird onto it. Using a tack, he pinned it above his bed, in line with his pillow. Dropping onto the mattress, he gazed up at the ceiling with a dreamy smile, reaching up and lightly knocking the bird with his finger before closing his eyes and drifting back to Helena's side.

30

Paper Cranes Can't Fly

As his father had predicted, Tristan didn't sleep well. He kept waking in the night, giddy butterflies rushing through him as he relived every second of his date with Helena. Yeah, he had it real bad...but he didn't care. He was in love, and it felt like nothing he'd ever experienced before.

Sitting up with a chuckle, he scratched his hair and straightened out the clothes he'd slept in. His plan of attack for the morning was to start researching ways to set Helena free.

Jumping through a quick shower, he brushed his teeth and headed downstairs. His father wasn't around, but that wasn't unusual. He always slept in on a Saturday. Tristan messed around in the kitchen, putting on some toast for himself and pouring a large glass of orange juice. He gulped it down while tapping his knife on the counter, waiting for his toast to pop.

His mind was racing, trying to decide where to start when he got back to his computer.

The toast popped and he pulled it free, dropping it on the plate with a light hiss and blowing on his fingertips. He eased the kitchen window open, letting a rush of cool air inside.

That's when he heard it.

A faint yelling.

He normally would have ignored it, but there was something about the tone, and the fact that he could hear it from inside his house. It was a screaming flurry of words...a symphony of rage.

His brow furrowed and he glanced out the window, wondering who was kicking up such a stink. Curiosity got the better of him and he reached for the back door, popping it open to see if he could hear better.

"You can't do this to me anymore!" A girl to his right screeched the words and Tristan's throat restricted.

Helena.

His heart beat in triple time and he raced out the door, trying to get a better view of the green house.

"Let go! How could you betray me this way!" the dragon roared.

Tristan whipped down the driveway, frantically searching the house for an open window, trying to figure out where they were arguing. He couldn't see the tower window from his angle, but it sounded like the shouts were coming from there.

That couldn't be right. It was bolted shut. He'd pound on the door until someone answered. He didn't care how long it took.

"I was safe. Nothing happened. He loves me, Mother. He wants to protect me. And I love him! I need to be with him!"

Tristan missed her mother's response, but hearing Helena wail "No!" like she was in some kind of pain tore him in half.

"He's tricked you! Turned you against me!"

Anger bubbled in Tristan's chest, snorts puffing out his nose as he shouldered the gate open and ran across the raggedy lawn. He was ready to stomp up those porch stairs and start pounding the door. He wasn't above giving that dragon a piece of his mind. He didn't care if she called the police. He wasn't letting her treat Helena this way.

"Helena!" the dragon screeched, fear lacing her tone. "What are you doing? Get back in here!"

Tristan froze. The panic in Mrs. Thompson's voice had rapid breaths punching out of him. He ran around the house and paused against the gate, gazing up at the tower.

"Let me go! You can't keep me from him!" Helena shouted.

Tristan's heart stopped beating as he saw Helena dangling out the window. Her legs hung in the air, kicking around as she tried to find her footing.

The dragon's arms came out the window, clutching at her daughter's hands. "Stop this madness at once!"

Helena flicked her hands, scratching at her mother's hold on her.

Tristan's eyes bulged wide as she kicked her legs and fought. "Stop," he breathed, barely able to say the words as he ran toward the base of the tower.

"Let me go!" Helena screamed again, her face bunching with fierce rage as she slapped at her mother's hands. The tips of her toes were balanced on the edge of the trellis, a precarious perch that would not hold her if she didn't stop struggling.

"Helena, hang on!" Tristan yelled, racing through the grass to reach her. "Stop fighting! I'll help you."

Fear pulsed through him, thrumming in his ears and nearly popping his brain when he heard Helena scream.

He skidded to a stop, staring up at the tower in horror as her body dropped through the air. Her long hair rose into the sky, hiding her face while her pale pink dress floated around her and she plummeted like a cannon ball.

"HELENA!"

Pumping his arms, Tristan sprinted to the bottom of the tower, but not before the thud.

The sickening, mind-numbing thud.

His stomach convulsed, his knees buckling as he dropped to the grass.

"No," he cried.

Crawling through the overgrown lawn, he scrambled to her side, tears already blinding him.

"Helena!" her mother screamed from the window above. "Stay away from her! Stay away!"

Tristan ignored the hollering, stopping next to Helena's motionless body. She'd landed on her back, her arms and legs spread as if she were floating in the water.

"Helena," he whispered, brushing the hair off her face.

"Tristan." She blinked up at the overcast sky, fear casting a shadow over her bright gaze. "Tristan." She puffed out his name before sucking in a terrified breath.

"It's okay. I'm here. I'm here." He brushed the hair off her face and kissed her forehead. "What hurts? Tell me how I can help you."

"I–I don't know."

"Is your head okay? Do you have any pain?"

She shook her head slowly, her hair rustling in the long grass. "I'm not sure. Everything is sort of numb."

"O-okay." He patted her leg, nervously tapping her thigh as he tried to get his horrified brain to think straight. He gave her leg a little squeeze and smiled down at her, but her face was white with terror.

"What?" He leaned over her, searching her expression for any kind of clue.

"What was that patting sound?" she choked. "Are you touching my leg?"

His hands flew off her. "I'm sorry, did that hurt?"

"I couldn't feel it." Her words wobbled while Tristan's mind went numb. Closing his eyes for a second, he laid his hand back down on her leg and gave it a firm squeeze.

He opened his eyes and whispered, "I just squeezed your thigh. Anything?"

"I can't—I can't...feel you." Her breath caught on the last word, a tear trickling out the side of her eye and gently rolling down her cheek.

The air in his lungs evaporated and it took him a minute to find his words. "It's... I'm gonna—I'm gonna call an ambulance, okay?" His voice was deep and trembling, unfamiliar to his ears. He sounded like he was talking through a mouthful of mud, the words coming out slow and hazy. "I have to go and get my phone."

"Don't leave me," she sobbed, her chin trembling. He'd never seen her so petrified. He pressed his lips to her forehead, unsure what else to do.

"Tristan?" His dad's voice reached him from over the fence.

"Dad, over here!" His head popped up, relief coursing through him. "Bring the phone! We need help!"

He reached for Helena's hand, gently lifting it and kissing her wrist. She squeezed back and hope skirted through him. "You can move your fingers." He tried to smile down at her. "It's okay. We're gonna get you help. Everything will be okay." He touched her cheek, leaning over her so she was forced to look into his eyes.

She blinked, sucking in a shaky breath, obviously trying to believe him.

He fought the tears that were clawing at his throat and trying to blind him.

"Get away from her! Get away!" Dragon lady appeared

around the corner, a baseball bat in her hand.

Tristan whipped around to see her coming, his eyes rounding. She raised the bat over her head and screamed like a banshee as she charged.

Tristan raised his arm to block the blow, but the bat was snatched before she could deliver the brutal swing. Her body stumbled back and she thumped down on her butt.

"Hey! That's my son!" Tristan's dad towered over the woman, puffing like a rhino as he yanked the bat out of her hand and hurled it across the yard. It spun a couple of times before clanking into a tree and being swallowed by the grass.

The feeble woman shrank away from him, her ferocious expression crumpling to a look of terror. She crab-crawled back in the long grass, her arms giving out quickly. Landing on her side near Helena's feet, she raked her gaze over her daughter, her blue eyes bright with liquid fear. Covering her mouth with a trembling hand, she let out a pitiful whine before disintegrating into a blubbering mess. Sobs punctured the air, making it hard to think straight.

Tristan leaned away from the crippling noise, wincing up at his father who was eyeing the woman with shocked disbelief. His gaze then traveled to Helena's broken body, his expression folding with sympathy.

"What happened?"

"She fell," Tristan croaked, pointing up at the tower window.

His father's lips parted, his brow wrinkling. "I'll call an

ambulance."

Yanking the phone from his back pocket, he dialed 9-1-1, spinning away from the heart-wrenching scene and pacing through the grass.

Tristan tuned out his father's deep voice as he gave them all the information. Helena was still staring up at the sky. Her chin trembled. Her fingers kept squeezing Tristan's hand as if to assure herself he was there.

"I won't leave you," he whispered, leaning his cheek against her head.

She didn't respond, just closed her eyes while her chest heaved.

Her mother's sobs eased, dying down to breathy hiccups as she crawled around to her daughter's side. Her fluttering hand rested on Helena's stomach.

"It's all right, sweetheart. I'll keep you safe." Her tender smile and soft voice could've fooled anyone into thinking she hadn't been the psychotic woman screaming at him less than five minutes earlier.

Tristan scowled at her. She caught his gaze and met it head-on, her blue glare enough to freeze his insides.

"Let go of my daughter." Her slow command was wrapped in steel.

Tristan gripped Helena's hand, his chin lifting in defiance. "She doesn't want me to."

"She doesn't know what she wants. Do you think this would have happened if you hadn't filled her head with lies?"

"Lies?"

"Please, stop." Helena's whisper was so soft Tristan

barely even registered it.

"You want to talk to me about lies! What the hell have you been feeding her for the last eight years? That the world's going to hurt her?"

"It has," the woman barked. "Look at her! If she hadn't been trying to sneak out to see you, she never would have fallen!"

Tristan had a rebuttal but it was locked in his throat, held down by an overwhelming guilt. He couldn't speak past it, couldn't even think past the idea that he'd started all of this. Before him, Helena had been safe and happy in her imaginary world...and now she was lying on the ground, most likely paralyzed, and the chances of her ever breaking free were shattered.

A siren wail filled the air. Curious neighbors peeked out their windows and stepped onto their driveways as the ambulance pulled to a stop outside the mysterious green house.

Tristan was forced to let Helena go, stepping away so the paramedics could do what was needed. His body was numb, his ears ringing with Mrs. Thompson's accusations.

Crossing his arms, he watched the paramedics brace Helena's body and roll her onto a board, working in a calm, efficient manner while her mother jittered around behind them. They carried Helena through the tall grass and out the gate, sliding her into the ambulance. The doors slammed shut and Helena was whisked away from him.

She never called out his name or asked him to follow,

so he stood by his father's side, a desolate statue.

The moment the ambulance pulled away, his father's hand landed on the back of Tristan's neck. He gave it a light squeeze and gently led him back to the house. Tristan moved like a wide-eyed robot, shuffling down his driveway and up the back stairs. As soon as they were inside the kitchen, his father pulled out a wooden chair and plunked Tristan into it.

Tristan slumped down, his eyes narrowing in on the knotted bit of wood in the middle of the table.

He heard the fridge door open and shut, then the clunk of a can being placed in front of him. Condensation dripped down the side. Tristan reached for it, rubbing his thumb over the white and red Coca-Cola symbol.

Popping the top, his father took a few large gulps before pulling a chair out and sitting down. His stare was intense and unrelenting, his head tipping to the side before he let out a slow sigh. "Okay, bud, time to start talking." He leaned forward, resting his elbows on his knees. "And I need every detail."

31

A Change of Roles

It drained him completely, but Tristan told his father everything, from the day he climbed through Helena's window to the moment she fell. His dad stayed silent for most of it, his eyes bulging over the part where the dragon lady turned books into missiles. Thankfully he kept his judgments to himself, sipping at his Coke and scratching his whiskers to try and hide his concern.

Tristan appreciated the effort.

"I never expected them to fight, and I *never* thought she'd try to sneak out the tower window." Tristan lurched back and grabbed two fistfuls of hair. "What was she thinking?"

"She probably wasn't. Intense emotion like that can make us do crazy things. You were the idiot who climbed a tower to get to her."

"Yeah, but, I...I could do it."

"You could have fallen just as easily." His father's face bunched with his broken whisper. "I can't even think about..." He sighed, running a shaky hand through his graying hair.

"I love her, Dad."

Leon's brown gaze was gentle when he looked at Tristan, a small half smile pushing at his lips. "It's about the only thing that can make us fly and plummet. Love is dangerous, but it's also magic."

"Was it my fault?" Tristan's breath caught, slicing into his question. His throat began to swell again, making it impossible to swallow.

"No." His father's hand landed on his knee and gave it a firm squeeze. "This is not your fault. She chose to climb through that window. You didn't make her."

"But I—"

"No." His father's thick index finger pointed at him, his emphatic gaze impossible to turn away from. "You are not allowed to do that to yourself. The only thing you did was make her love you enough to want to be with you. That's not something to be ashamed of."

Tristan pressed his lips together, finally managing to swallow.

"I wish I could have kept your mother. If I could turn

back time, I would..." He sighed. "I would have done it all differently. You have to cherish this girl. She needs to know that you're there for her."

Tristan scoffed, clenching his jaw while tears tried to burn him. "I can't. I can't even reach her now. If she's paralyzed..." Tristan let out a sick groan, leaning forward and holding his head in his hands.

"Then she'll deal with it and she'll learn to live a new kind of life."

Tristan's jaw locked, tears quaking his words. "But her mother...she'll never let her out of the house again. There'll be no chance of her seeking help or getting out in the world. She'll lock them both away."

"We don't know that yet." His father's large hand landed on his shoulder, giving it a firm squeeze. "Come on, let's go to the hospital. We'll find out what we can."

Tristan gazed up at his father. "Seriously?"

"Yeah, let's go." He jumped out of his seat, racing out of the room to get changed and grab his keys.

Tristan pulled on his boots, struggling to tie the laces as he waited for his father. The urge to get to the hospital was battling with the urge to bury himself inside a hole. He didn't know what state Helena would be in when he got there. Would she want to see him? What could he possibly say to make it better?

The drive to the hospital was pure torture. Tristan's leg bobbed the whole time, the toe of his boot pressing into the dash. His father knew better than to say anything, so he kept his eyes on the road and his lips sealed. They found a spot easily and bustled into the emergency room.

Tristan raced for the counter, slamming into it and startling the nurse on duty.

"Sorry," he mumbled. "I'm here to see a friend."

"Name?" She gave him a droll look.

"Uh, Helena...Thompson. She came in about an hour ago."

"Mmhmm." The woman clicked at her keyboard, adjusting her reading glasses to stare at the screen. "And how are you related to the patient?"

"A friend."

"Son." She removed her glasses, folding her arms across her ample chest and shaking her head. "I can't let you through."

"But I need to see her." He tipped his head.

"She's his girlfriend," Dad piped up over Tristan's shoulder.

The woman's face bunched with a look of sympathy and she rose from her chair with a sigh. "I can ask, but don't hold your breath."

"Thank you." Tristan leaned against the counter as she walked away, gripping the shiny edge in an attempt to stay standing.

His father hovered behind him, a towering pillar of

strength. It was kind of ironic really, the whole change of situation. He'd never expected his dad to step up, but he had. It made him want to cry with relief.

Ten minutes ticked by with a slow painfulness that made Tristan's head pound. Patients shuffled in and out of the ER, phones rang, wheels squeaked on shiny floors, and static voices blurted from the intercom. Finally the woman reappeared, her sympathetic friendliness replaced with a stern look of reprimand.

"You are not welcome to visit Miss Thompson, and my suggestion to you is that you leave right now."

"But—" Tristan lifted his hand, an argument at the ready.

"I've spoken to her mother, so don't try any tricks with me." She pointed an accusing finger at Tristan.

"This is bull—"

"Sir, I will call security if I need to." She snatched the phone from the cradle, her big eyes rounding with assertion.

"You don't." His father's voice matched the firm hand on Tristan's shoulder. With a little squeeze, he pulled his son away from the desk and led him back outside.

The glass door shut behind them and Tristan kicked the concrete ramp leading out of the hospital entrance. "This is horse shit!"

Ripping off his beanie, he squeezed it in his hands, trying to fight the overwhelming urge to punch something.

"I know." His father sighed, shoving his hands into his pockets and leaning against the metal railing.

"I just want to know if she's okay. I need to see her."

"I know you do." His dad's brows dipped together and he looked over his shoulder, scanning their surroundings with narrowed eyes.

"What are you thinking?" Tristan twisted the beanie in his hands.

"I'm thinking we're not leaving here until you see your girl...and I'm thinking this is a pretty big hospital and there's probably more than one way in and out."

Tristan's lips twitched with a surprised smile. Was his father seriously saying that stuff to him?

His dad's half grin grew as he stood forward and lightly punched Tristan's arm. "Come on, let's try around this way."

32

Desolation

Sneaking in ended up being easier than Tristan thought. His father led him around the back and he snuck in through a delivery door. The white sterile lights reflected off the clean, squeaky floor as he scurried through the bowels of the hospital. Finding an elevator, he caught it to the first floor and peeked his head out. The coast was clear of anyone he knew, so he stepped out, merging with a large family holding balloons and a bunch of flowers.

He scanned the signs as he went, leaving the group

and ducking into the shadows outside the emergency ward. He was pretty sure Helena would still be in there.

Crouching low, he snuck to the door, popping up to peer inside the round windows. He couldn't see much, just rows of beds, some with curtains pulled around them.

A tall male nurse in blue scrubs and white sneakers came into view, moving for the door. Tristan pressed himself against the wall, hiding behind the door and then catching it with his hand once the nurse had bustled through.

He crept into the room, his eyes darting around the area while the intense smell of the sterile environment stung his nostrils. Aware that his sneaky tiptoeing might seem suspicious, he pulled his shoulders back and tried to saunter, casually stopping by each curtain and peeking inside.

Helena was in the third bed down, and by some act of providence was actually alone.

Tristan's breath caught as he gazed at her. She looked pale, her usually bright eyes dull and lifeless as they stared up at the ceiling. Her long hair was draped over one shoulder and her thin hands were clasped together. His gaze fluttered over her legs beneath the blanket. An acidic bile swirled in his stomach.

She probably didn't even want to see him.

Closing his eyes, he clutched the curtain and contemplated leaving when a soft whisper stopped him. "Tristan?"

"Hey." He forced a smile, tiptoeing to her side and resting his hand on top of hers.

"How did you get in here?"

"I snuck in." He cringed. "I had to see you."

Her lips toyed with a smile, rising at the edges for the briefest moment before starting to quiver.

"Hey." His voice was a gentle caress. He leaned over her, kissing her cheek and pressing his forehead against hers. Her jasmine scent was being tainted by the sterile smell of the emergency ward. He closed his eyes, squeezing her hands lightly. "It's going to be okay."

"How?" she whispered.

He leaned away, gazing down at her stricken expression. "I don't know. But I *do* know you're strong and you can survive this."

"I might not be able to walk ever again. I'll never dance, never be able to climb the attic stairs," she whimpered. "I can't reach my haven anymore."

"You don't need that haven." He kissed the tears trying to escape out the corner of her eye. "You can take your imagination wherever you go...and you'll learn. You'll learn to walk again. They have ways to teach you. This isn't over."

"It should be." She wiggled her hands from beneath his grasp.

His fingers fell to the blanket, rubbing over the coarse white covering. He glanced down, his eyebrows dipping as he pinched the blanket.

"Whether I walk again or not, this is going to be a long, slow process, and you can't be tied to me. Mother blames you for this. She won't let you near, and it's only going to make things worse. In her eyes, the outside world has hurt me. She'll trap me forever...and I can't trap you as well."

"Don't say that." Tristan shook his head. "Please, I don't—I don't want to live without you."

Her despair fled for a moment, replaced with a warm glow. Reaching for his face, she cupped his cheek and whispered. "Sweet, Tristan. Only knights of old talk that way."

"That's what I am." He sniffed. "A sentimental fool, just like Romeo."

She shook her head, her laughter sounding hollow and sad. "She caught me unbolting the tower window. I'd found a screwdriver in the closet. I thought maybe I could secretly escape and then climb back up after I'd seen you. But she walked in and...and then she saw my necklace. Asked me where it had come from." Helena swallowed. "I couldn't lie, so I told her. I relived the night in my dreamy splendor, unaware of the way her eyes glazed over, the mottled tone of her skin. She ripped the necklace from me. Told me I would never see you again." Tears built on Helena's lashes. "All I could think about was escaping and being with you." Her lips wobbled, her chin bunching as the tears descended. "But that can never happen now, so I must set you free."

"No." Tristan frowned. "I don't want to be set free. I want to be with you, no matter what."

Helena ignored him, her gaze distant as she stared at the ceiling. "Juliet didn't have to kill herself, you know. She could have lived...fallen in love again."

Tristan stood tall, hating the turn of the conversation.

"Come on, where's the romance in that?" He put on a brave smile, shoving his hands in his pockets and rocking back on his heels.

Helena pressed her lips together, her chin trembling when she met his gaze. "You have to live, Tristan. You have to make every heartbeat count, and you can't do that if you're trying to help me. I want your house filled with paper cranes."

"They will be. They'll be filled with *our* paper cranes. We'll write them together."

Shaking her head, she opened her mouth to deny him, but he lurched forward and stopped her words with his soft lips. She quivered against his touch, sucking in a whimper as she reached for his head and threaded her fingers into his thick locks.

He pulled back, breathing against her skin. "We can do this."

"You shouldn't have to."

"But I want to." He pulled back a little more so they could look each other in the eye. "I'll fight for us. Whatever it takes...and...and you want to leave a footprint, remember? Even if you can't walk, you can still leave your mark. I'll help you do it."

"It was a pipe dream, Tristan, and I can't expect you to burden yourself with me. It's too hard." She sucked in a breath, her raspy whisper barely audible. "She'll win and I'll disappear."

Her blue eyes shone with fear.

"No, you won't. I'm not—"

The curtain snapped back, making them both flinch.

Helena gasped. Her wild gaze flicked from her mother to Tristan, her large eyes rounding so wide it hurt. Tristan reached for her hand, giving it a reassuring rub.

It was the wrong move.

The dragon's eyes flashed. "What are you doing in here? Get away from her."

Yanking at his jacket, she tugged him back from the bed, yelling for security.

"I just wanted to make sure she was okay," Tristan murmured.

"She's not okay. Can't you see that? She'll never be okay again, thanks to you." Her dark words dripped with accusation.

Tristan flinched, like she'd physically slapped him.

"No, Mother. That's not fair." Helena wasn't loud enough to cut through the woman's animosity.

"Please, just leave us." The desperate request distorted her mother's voice, making it sound deep and heavy.

Tristan stumbled back from the bed and straight into a pissed off security guard. The man snatched his arm and Tristan didn't fight him.

Glancing at the bed, Tristan drank in Helena's desolate expression and whispered, "Fight for us."

Her eyes shone with tears and she shook her head, cutting their connection by closing her eyes.

The security guard yanked Tristan away before he could say any more, and a deep sorrow pulled him down as he trudged out of the hospital.

33

A Dose of Miss Warren

Tristan's father couldn't console him. They drove home in silence. As soon as he was in the door, Tristan trooped up to his room and remained there. He didn't want to eat and he couldn't sleep, woken by constant dreams of Helena's body falling to the ground—the way her hair fluttered around her face...and then the thud.

The morning brought no relief, so he stayed beneath the covers staring at the paper cranes above him and lamenting the fact that he may never have anymore. His father knocked on his door late in the morning, holding two baseball mitts.

"You want to play catch?"

He frowned at his father's pitiful attempt, shaking his head and rolling away without a word. He waited out the sigh and the slow click of his door closing before getting out of bed. There were still a few paper cranes sitting on his desk. Snatching a marker, he wrote down his woes on the wings and threw them out the window.

Pressing his palms against the frame, he watched them float on the breeze and land in the gutter.

"It didn't work," he muttered. "I still feel like shit."

He squeezed his eyes shut, pinching the bridge of his nose and shuffling back to bed.

Although he wanted to stay there for a few more days, his father wouldn't let him. At six thirty the next morning, his covers were thrown back and he was ordered into the shower. Seeing his father take control again was a weird experience. Tristan couldn't decide if he liked it or not.

"I'm driving you to school," his father murmured, sipping at his coffee before taking a bite from his toast.

"I've got my bike," Tristan muttered.

"Your brain is on another planet today and I don't trust you in the traffic. Let me drive you to school and pick you up."

Tristan's eyebrows bunched together and he pushed his bowl of half-eaten Cheerios away.

His father stopped the bowl from falling off the table and threw Tristan a disapproving frown. "Okay, I get it. You're not used to me playing dad, but it's my turn. You looked after me when my heart was in pieces. Now I've got to step up and do the same for you, so please let me, okay?"

Tristan shrugged, gazing down at the table and avoiding eye contact.

It was probably horrible for his father, but Tristan had suffered the same stony silence for months, so it was only fair.

Rising from the breakfast table, he threw out his cereal, rinsed the bowl, and then got ready for school. They pulled into the Burlington High parking lot and Tristan got out of his dad's pickup truck with a mumbled goodbye. He could feel his father staring at his back the whole way into school, but he wasn't about to turn around and wave.

Jumping straight back to his old tricks, Tristan fell into numb mode, letting the world around him turn to fuzz. He missed the concern in Mikayla's voice when she asked him how his weekend was, and he nearly got hit in the head with a flying football on his way to PE.

He remained in a dazed stupor until the end of English when Miss Warren pulled him up after class.

"What is it this time?" he muttered, kicking at the desk leg and bumping it out of alignment. He gripped his bag strap, feeling bad but not making a move to correct his mistake.

"You've got that lifeless look in your eyes again."

Tristan shrugged.

Miss Warren crossed her arms, her skin-colored pumps tapping on the floor as she walked around to the front of her desk. She leaned her butt against it and tipped her head to study him. "How's your friend?"

Tristan's face bunched. He didn't want to talk about it, but the soft way she asked was bending his will. He sucked in a sharp breath, bunching his lips and looking away from her.

"Uh-oh," she whispered. "What happened?"

"She had an accident." He swallowed, running a hand through his hair and fighting the burn of tears. "She fell and now she's in the hospital. They think she might be...paralyzed." The last word nearly choked him. He struggled to clear his throat and remain standing. His legs were quivering inside his jeans.

"Oh, Tristan, I'm so sorry."

"She can't be." His forehead crinkled. "She can't. She hasn't even lived yet. She hasn't experienced all the world has to offer. She wants to leave a footprint, but she won't let me help her do it."

Confusion marred Miss Warren's pretty face.

Tristan sucked in a shaky breath. "She's had a very sheltered life. I'd finally convinced her that there was more. She wanted to be a part of it, but now..."

"Now it's going to be a thousand times harder."

He nodded, biting his lips together and gazing down at the linoleum floor.

Miss Warren stepped forward, her shoes sounding loud in the empty room. He watched them approach—elegant, even steps—until she was standing in front of him. She squeezed his shoulder. "Harder, but not impossible. She'll learn to experience life in a different way."

"No she won't." He shook his head. "You don't know... She—" He glanced up at his sympathetic teacher, wanting to tell her but unable to find the words.

He let out a ragged sigh, fisting his bag strap.

"I promised her she'd always exist somehow. I promised her that I'd always keep her with me, but I don't know how I'm gonna do that when she wants me to leave her. She wants me to get on with my life, without her."

Miss Warren's brown eyes were soft with compassion. "That's obviously what she needs right now to cope. But she might change her mind."

"I just want her to be happy. I want to give her some sense of hope in all of this. I can't do that if I'm not there."

Miss Warren's eyes grew warm as she smiled at him. "Tristan, you're new here and I'm still getting to know you, but what I have learned is that you're a guy with a really big heart. If anyone can find a way to help this girl, it's you. Keep your distance if that's what she wants you to do, but don't give up. You'll find a way to bring her hope, I just know it."

34

The Perfect Poem

Miss Warren's words were comforting, uplifting even, but the emotion didn't last for long. The next morning he biked to school, heavy with Helena's burden. The look of fear on her face when she said it was over haunted him. He couldn't let that be their last encounter. He couldn't let her think that he'd just walk away so easily.

He needed to see her again, but it was risky, and the visit had to mean something. It had to be magical, epic, the kind of visit worthy of Helena's romantic heart.

Mikayla slapped her locker shut, snapping Tristan out

of his daydream. "Look, I know you don't want to talk about whatever's bothering you. It's not your way or whatever, but Tristan, I'm here if you need me, okay?"

Her words were slow to register. Gazing down at her petite face, he forced a smile, feeling bad for continually ignoring her. For someone so small, she sure had a lot of determination. She wasn't giving up on him anytime soon.

He wanted to tell her to stop wasting her time. He wasn't friend material, but he was pretty sure the statement would hurt her feelings and he didn't have it in him to damage anyone else.

"Thanks," Tristan mumbled, brushing past her and heading for the cafeteria. He didn't feel like eating, but his stomach was telling him otherwise. He'd grab a quick bite and then go hide out in a quiet part of the school.

"Mr. Parker," Miss Warren called down the corridor. People around him shot curious glances over their shoulders as his English teacher wove her way through the lunchtime traffic.

He edged to the side, finding a small pocket of space against the wall.

Her smile was sweet and motherly as she approached him. "I couldn't stop thinking about your friend last night. Your story really touched me. What you want to do for her is...beautiful, even if she doesn't want your help right now."

Tristan managed a half smile and nod of thanks, dropping his gaze to the floor when a trio of jocks passed them. The big one muttered something and the other two snickered. Tristan bit the inside of his cheek.

"Anyway..." Miss Warren spread her hands. "I thought of a solution for how you could keep your promise and respect her wishes at the same time." She held out a brown leather book. "I don't understand everything that's going on, but I do know this could bring her the peace she's looking for."

Tristan stared at the cover, his face bunching with confusion.

She smiled. "I want you to borrow this. It's a collection of poetry by E.E. Cummings."

She shook it, encouraging him to reach forward and collect the offering. With a tentative hand, he took it from her, running his fingers over the title imprint.

"It's a first edition, so be careful with it." She winked.

He shot it back towards her hand. "I can't. This is too precious."

She crossed her arms, refusing to take it back. "It's only a loan, and trust me, you want this book. It might hold the answer you're looking for."

He frowned in confusion.

"It's one of his 1952 poems...about the heart. You'll know it when you see." She winked.

Rendered speechless, Tristan watched his teacher spin on her heel and clip back to her classroom. A few curious onlookers gave him quizzical stares. He ignored them, brushing through the crowd and heading to the library. Lunch could wait.

Sneaking into the quiet space, he headed for a table in the back corner and perched his elbows on the polished wood.

He thumbed through the old pages and found the collection of poems Miss Warren was talking about. He scanned for the word *heart* and found the title easily. He figured it must be the one she was talking about. Opening the book wide, he winced as the spine crackled, but then he started reading. He began mumbling the words, and then his lips parted with wonder before rising into a very slow smile.

Placing the book on the table, he spread his hand over the old pages and leaned back in his chair. It was a great promise. It was full and emotional and said way more than a sixteen-year-old should.

Tapping his finger over the text, he pursed his lips. Giving it to her would be a huge commitment on his part, but he'd want to follow through. He didn't want the decision to be spontaneous and based on emotion. When he gave her the poem, he wanted to mean every single word.

Pulling the book off the table, he read the text again.

"*And this is the wonder that's keeping the stars apart*," he murmured, his smile growing again.

Yeah, decision made. He had to give Helena this poem, and he had to give it to her that day. Snatching his bag off the floor, he pulled out a sheet of blank paper and a black pen.

Going slow, he copied out the text in his best handwriting and blew on the ink to dry it. He was about to fold it like a standard letter but paused before making the first crease. With a playful grin, he set about folding the paper with a little more meaning. His face bunched with concentration, his eyebrows making a tight V as he fumbled through the task.

Pressing his hand over the creation, he shook his head and muttered, "That'll have to do."

The end of lunch bell rang and Tristan looked over his shoulder at the clock on the wall.

He'd never played hooky before in his life, but there was no way he'd be able to concentrate anyway.

Hitching his bag onto his shoulder, he sauntered out of the library and snuck out of school. His hands shook as he unlocked his bike, praying he wouldn't get busted. As soon as the lock was free, he jumped on his bike and started pedaling.

It didn't matter what kind of trouble awaited him the next day...or even at the hospital. The only thing that mattered was giving Helena a paper crane.

35

I'll Carry Your Heart

Tristan locked up his bike and walked into the hospital, trying to look as though he belonged there. Ambling up to the counter, he shone the receptionist a pleasant smile and asked which room Helena Thompson was in. She looked it up and told him visiting hours finished at seven.

He nodded and headed for the elevator, nerves skittering through him. His hands shook as he pushed the button for the third floor. It took two attempts before the button lit. He rode up with an old man who kept sniffing and a lady with spiral curls whose nails tapped on her phone screen the entire time. He stared at his shoes until the elevator dinged.

Ducking into the corridor, he headed for the neurology ward and room ten. He slowed down near the door and peeked inside, sucking in a breath and ducking out of sight. Mrs. Thompson was by the bed, leaning back in her chair and staring at her daughter with a desolate expression.

Tristan didn't get a chance to see Helena's face, just the tips of her feet beneath the blankets. He scuttled back down the hallway, setting up position against the wall—out of sight, yet with a clear view of the door.

All he had to do was wait until Mrs. Thompson left the room.

He rolled his eyes. That could take forever, but surely she'd have to use the bathroom at some point.

Leaning his shoulder against the wall, he shoved his hands in his pockets. The crane crumpled beneath his touch and he winced, pulling it out and trying to resurrect the dented bird. It really was a pitiful attempt, but it held more meaning than anyone could fathom.

Helena would get it though.

His lips twitched with a smile.

"Excuse me, young man?"

Tristan glanced up at the soft voice and jerked tall, clearing his throat and running a hand through his hair.

A nurse with light mocha skin and jet-black curls stared at him curiously.

"Are you waiting for someone?" She slid her pen into

her green scrubs pocket.

"Just visiting a friend," he croaked.

Following his line of sight, she glanced over her shoulder and then turned back with a knowing grin.

"I see." Her lips pursed to the side, but then broke into an easy grin. "Your name wouldn't happen to be Tristan, would it?"

He licked his bottom lip, dreading what was about to come. Before she could kick him out, he stepped forward, his face creasing with a pleading look. "I just want to talk to her for a minute. I swear I won't stay long."

"There's no way you're going to get past her mother."

He slumped back against the wall with a sigh.

"But I'll see what I can do." She winked.

He frowned, his head tipping with the silent question.

She chuckled and shook her head. "That girl in there has it pretty bad for you. Apparently she murmured your name throughout the night, and when I caught her crying this morning she confessed a little. I think it'd do her good to see you."

His blue eyes sparkled as he mouthed, "Thank you."

"Don't thank me yet. We still need to get security out of the room." Her eyes rounded with a comical look that made Tristan snicker. "Wish me luck."

Tristan shifted on his feet, resting his butt against the wall and gripping the insides of his pockets.

It was a nervous ten minutes, but eventually the nurse popped out with Mrs. Thompson.

"I really shouldn't leave her."

"Ma'am, you will do your daughter no service by

starving yourself. You head on down to the cafeteria. I'll keep an eye on her for you. There's nothing to worry about."

"I'll just be fifteen minutes." Mrs. Thompson's voice trembled. She looked so small and fragile next to the robust nurse.

"You take your time."

Mrs. Thompson stopped and gazed back at the door.

"Please, Mrs. Thompson. Do this for Helena. She needs you strong and well in order to face this journey ahead."

The woman's eyes rounded, her chest sinking in as her shoulders slumped.

"I suppose you're right," she finally whispered, sucking in a fearful breath. "I'll be back shortly."

The nurse gave her a tight smile, ushering her towards the elevators. Tristan turned his head as they walked past, but as soon as the coast was clear, he darted into Helena's room.

She was gazing out the window, her pale face on the pillow looking fragile and lost. Her brow creased and she closed her eyes, swallowing slowly before inching them back open.

Tristan's heart spasmed as he clutched the end of the metal bed.

"Hey," he whispered, managing a half smile that would hopefully hide his anguish.

With a sweet gasp, she whipped around to face him, her eyes lighting and her lips rising into a weak smile.

"You came back." Her laugh was breathy and

surprised. "I wasn't sure if you would."

He stepped around the bed, perching his butt on the side and gently taking her hand. Lifting it to his lips, he kissed her knuckles. "Of course I came back. I couldn't let that be the last time I saw you."

Her expression was sweet and tender, her jade eyes trying to shine, yet not quite making it. That low-lying fear still remained.

"How are you?" He rubbed his thumb over the back of her hand.

She sucked in a shaky breath. "Mother desperately wants me back in our castle. She won't stop talking about it. Her anxiety is growing more each day. She's been arguing with doctors over whether or not she should allow me to undergo surgery. She's convinced the anesthetic will kill me. The doctors aren't pleased and insist I stay here for further testing and observation."

"Will the surgery help you walk again?"

"They're not sure." Helena shrugged. "They say I have a lumbar spinal fracture. An operation might help, but there are no guarantees." Her voice caught on the last word.

"But if there's even a chance, you have to take it." Tristan frowned.

"I'm only fifteen. I need her consent."

"But it's your—"

She raised her hand to silence him. "You don't have to argue with me. I know it's my body, and I should have a say. But she's sick, remember? She can't hear reason like the rest of us can." Closing her eyes, she leaned her head back against the pillows with a weary sigh. "There have been so many phone calls and whispered conversations outside the door. No one will give me a definitive answer, and I don't know what's going on." Her lips wobbled. "It frightens me."

He squeezed her hand but she wriggled her fingers free, running them down her long braid and picking up the end. She wound the hair around her finger, her small nose twitching while her chin trembled.

"I don't like this fear, Tristan. I don't want to live like this, but I can't seem to find any kind of light or hope in this brewing darkness. All I see before me is despair."

His face crumpled and he took her hand back, pressing it against his cheek. "I wish I could make it better. I wish I could change it."

She gave him a sad smile. "There's nothing you can do. What's done is done and I will learn to live with it. It's not like much will really change. I already spend my life trapped in a house." Her voice petered away, the last few words only just audible.

"It doesn't have to stay that way."

"Oh, Tristan, stop it." She looked away from him, gazing out the window. Two birds were playing on the sill, their tiny feet bobbing up and down before their wings spread and they dashed into the air.

Helena swallowed. "I have to learn to accept my fate. Empty promises of hope won't help me do that." She wouldn't meet his gaze, her face awash with despair. "It won't take away the dread...the crushing reality." She sucked in a ragged breath, her eyes firmly fixed on the window. The light shining through was pale and dull, the sky a sad blue. "You should probably go before Mother returns."

Tristan stood from the bed, dropping her hand with a light sigh.

He checked the door and then looked down at the girl he loved. His heart swelled with agony before cresting with an overwhelming desire to take her fears away.

"I—I brought you a gift."

Her smile was small but instant, lighting her expression before she had time to stop it. "What is it?"

Digging into his pocket with a nervous snicker, he pulled out his feeble excuse for a paper crane.

"Sorry it's not folded very well." He winced as he handed it to her.

She took it, gently fingering the wings. "It's beautiful." She held it up to her eyes, frowning at the scrawled writing. "I can't read the words."

"Oh, I wrote a poem on the paper and then folded it."

A familiar sparkle danced in her eyes when she looked at him. "You wrote me a poem?"

"Well." Tristan tipped back on his heels with a bashful chuckle. "I didn't actually write it, I just copied it, but it's...it's like a promise." He looked down at her legs, running his fingers gently over the white hospital blanket. "Because no matter what happens, whether you have surgery or not or...even if you never walk again...or if your mother traps you in that big green house, I'm going to help you leave a footprint."

His eyes flicked up to meet her gaze. Her pale-faced

wonder was beautiful.

"How?" she whispered.

"It's in the poem." He cleared his throat and sat down, rubbing his hand up her thigh.

"Can you read it to me?" She passed him the crane.

"Uh." He gazed at the crane, nerves skittering through him. He wasn't one for reading aloud, especially a poem like that. He was kind of hoping she'd read it once he'd gone.

A family group walked passed the door, their wave of laughter catching Tristan's ears and making him spin to take a look. For a second he thought her mother was coming back, but it was safe. No one was coming in and he had no excuses not to follow through on her request.

"O-okay." He gingerly took the crane and unfolded it, careful not to rip the paper. He flattened it out against his chest, his cheeks burning with color. Scratching his chin, he cleared his throat again, glancing up to peek at her face.

A closed-mouth smile was perched on her lips, her eyes brimming with a look of adoration.

Shuffling on the bed, he held the paper in his hands, trying to ignore the way it trembled. He scanned the first line and opened his mouth to speak, but nothing came out.

The pads of her fingers brushed his hand, skimming over the skin and forcing the words from him.

"*I carry your heart with me,*" he croaked, his voice husky and foreign. Clearing the tickle from his throat, he shook his head and softly smiled at her. "*I carry it in my heart. I am never without it. Anywhere I go you go, my dear; And whatever is done by only me is your doing, my darling."* He swallowed, his eyes starting to smart as a tremor shook his voice. *"I fear no fate – for you are my fate, my sweet. I want no world – for beautiful you are my world, my true."*

Her fingers pressed into his hand and he looked at her, the glistening in her eyes making him want to cry. He sniffed and gazed back at the paper, refusing to look at her again. He'd never make it through the poem if he did.

Shifting his shoulders, he found his place and continued reading.

"And it's you are whatever a moon has always meant, and whatever a sun will always sing is you. Here is the deepest secret nobody knows. Here is the root of the root and the bud of the bud and the sky of the sky of a tree called life; Which grows higher than the soul can hope or mind can hide." His voice caught. Pressing his lips together, he sucked in a breath, ignoring the tear gliding down his cheek. *"And this is the wonder that's keeping the stars apart...I carry your heart. I carry it in my heart."*

He swiped at his tears and sniffed, feeling like a fool as he dropped the paper onto her legs. A few fresh trails trickled out the corner of his eyes, dripping down his nose. He sniffed again and rubbed them away with his knuckle.

"That's your promise to me?" Her voice shook and he had to break his resolve and take in her watery smile and quivering chin.

He nodded, unable to speak as emotion clogged his throat.

She let out a little chuckle, tears streaming down to her chin as she reached for his face. He leaned into her, letting her capture his cheeks and gaze into his eyes with a look of pure love so strong and true that he forgot how to breathe.

"Then I don't need to be afraid anymore," she whispered. "No matter what happens, you'll carry me."

"Always."

Her gratitude made her face shine, like a radiant light that Tristan was pulled towards. Their lips met in a kiss that belonged in fairytales—to knights and princesses, to the kind of love Romeo and Juliet died for.

Tristan cherished it, wrapping his brain around the feeling of her lips, the sweet smell of jasmine wafting up his nostrils, and the overpowering emotion charging through him.

36

Young Love

Tristan floated out of the room a minute before Mrs. Thompson returned. He'd promised Helena to return after school the next day to check on her. On his way to the elevator he glanced at the nurses' station, raising his hand in thanks. The nurse behind the counter nodded and winked at him, her face going soft with a dreamy smile.

She obviously believed in young love...like he did.

Hopefully she'd be working the next day. He needed an ally to get into Helena's room again.

Breathing in a lungful of air, Tristan looked to the ceiling as he traveled down to the ground floor. The weight of the past few days still lingered, but it didn't hurt so much. Helena had a long road ahead of her and he probably couldn't be there for all of it, but he'd take her heart with him wherever he went. He was determined to win her mother over somehow, so he could be a part of Helena's recovery. He wasn't sure how he'd do it, but he figured he'd chat with his dad and see what they could come up with together.

The idea sat right inside of him and he smiled the whole way home.

For once he was glad to see his dad's truck as he parked his bike in the garage. As soon as he walked into the house, he grabbed the mitts off the spare armchair and turned off the TV.

"Can we talk?" He threw the mitt at his father, who caught it against his stomach. A slow grin eased across the older man's face and he rose from the chair, catching the baseball in his hand and walking for the back door.

They played catch in their bare backyard until the sun went down, the whole time chatting about Tristan's dilemma. His father had a few good ideas, but all of them would be slow, time-consuming endeavors.

"There's not going to be a quick fix, buddy. You just have to accept that."

Tristan squeezed the baseball in his mitt with a frown. His father slapped his shoulder as they headed back inside.

"Are you sure you want to commit to her this way? It's

a big decision."

"I love her, Dad." He shrugged. "I know I'm young and she won't let me just kick around here looking after her, but she's the one, you know? She's going to be part of my life forever."

His dad grinned, nudging him with his elbow.

They walked into the house and made peanut butter and jelly sandwiches for dinner, his father going on about what a romantic sap Tristan had become.

Tristan laughed off the ribbing, happy to see his father's lighter side showing through again. Maybe he would be okay after all.

By nine o'clock, Tristan was exhausted. He shuffled off to bed, staring through the darkness at his paper cranes, the heavy weight of his future pressing in on him again. He was getting ahead of himself, but the idea of leaving Helena to go off and live his life hurt. It felt selfish. At least he could stay in Burlington to attend college, and then after that...well, he'd reassess. He didn't have to leave Burlington and go off exploring. Even after his promise to take her heart wherever he went...maybe that could just mean college classes. He didn't need to go off on some big adventure. He wanted to be able to see Helena every day, tell her about the mundane things in life. He could leave her footprint on campus somehow. Hell, maybe he could even take her with him.

There's no way her mother would let that happen.

He thumped the mattress with his fist.

Man, it was going to be challenging. But he wouldn't give up.

She was worth any fight...any sacrifice.

As soon as the final bell rang the next day, Tristan raced to his bike. He ignored Mikayla calling his name, jumping down the stairs and wrestling with his bike lock. He pedaled hard and made it to the hospital in record time. He couldn't wait to see his girl, kiss her lips, and remind her of his promise. He'd remind her every day if he had to.

Waltzing through the hospital with a bounce in his step, he walked straight to the elevators and rode up alone. The doors pinged open and he stepped out, heading for room ten, only to find it empty.

His brow furrowed and he spun around, walking for the nurses' station. The nurse from the day before was on duty again. He approached her with a smile that vanished the second he registered her face.

Her expression broke, her warm helpful smile disintegrating with a look of such utter heartache Tristan didn't want to face it.

"Helena?" he whispered, his heart starting to tremble in his chest.

The nurse swallowed, a loud audible sound as she guided him to the vinyl chairs lined up against the wall. Her hand was light on his shoulder, in contrast to the heavy sadness swirling around her.

He plunked into his seat, the buzz and hustle of the hospital fading to blackness when the nurse started talking.

"I don't know all the details, and if I'm not careful I could get fired for telling you this much."

"Where is she?"

"They arrived late last night, after my shift had ended. Apparently there was a big blowout, but her family was insistent. They left with her this morning."

"Family? What family?"

"From England. Her grandparents arrived...and..."

"What?" Tristan could barely breathe out the word.

"Like I said, I don't know all the details, but when Mrs. Thompson wouldn't listen to reason about her daughter's surgery, someone from the hospital contacted her next of kin to check on the woman's mental stability. It's the first step before taking things to Department of Children and Families. We've been noticing signs of paranoia and staff were concerned for Helena's well-being."

The nurse glanced over her shoulder like she was checking the coast was clear before turning back to Tristan.

"I'm sorry I can't tell you more, but her bed was empty before I even got to work. I'm only telling you what I've heard from the other nurses."

"But—" He started panting, like the air in his lungs wasn't good enough. He fought for more while his brain turned to sludge. "Is she... Did they take... *Where* did they take her?"

"Tristan, I'm sorry. I don't know for certain. My guess is that they've taken her back to England to continue her medical treatment there."

He spun in her seat, gripping her hand and silently pleading, "Where in England? Can you find out for me? Can you..."

"No." She spoke softly, her smile sad yet kind. "I've already told you more than I should have. Even if I dig out the records for you, we'll only have her sign-out information. I can't give you a specific address."

"Family name?"

"Tristan, her mother signed her out. I have no details that will help you."

His fight for air became that much harder. He felt like he was drowning in quicksand. He slumped forward, his elbows hitting his knees with a faint smack.

The nurse's hand landed on his back, rubbing lightly. "Do you need me to call someone?"

Tristan shook his head, numbness working through his system.

Helena was gone. She was...

Maybe she wasn't in England yet. Maybe they'd gone home to collect her things first!

Jerking from his seat, Tristan swallowed down the nausea tearing at his throat. "I gotta go." He choked out the words, lurching for the elevator.

The nurse trailed behind him. He could hear her soft patter as she followed him to the elevator.

"Are you sure you're going to be okay? You look like

you're about to pass out."

He stepped into the elevator, pressing the button multiple times. It click-click-clicked as he stood their panting.

"Tristan? Will you be all right?" she repeated.

He shook his head, his eyes burning. "Not until I find her."

The elevator doors slid shut and he closed his eyes, pressing his forehead against the metal. All he could hear was his heartbeat thrumming in his ears—a hollow, tinny sound that was trying to deafen him.

Stumbling to his bike, he tore home. His vision was blurry as he pedaled to Booth Street. He wanted to move like The Flash, but his legs were cast iron, his fingers brittle sticks as he clutched the handlebars.

He swerved into his driveway, dropping the bike in the middle of the concrete and rushing to the tall green fence. Shouldering open the gate, he ran to the house, yelling, "Helena!"

He sounded like a madman, but he didn't care.

Pounding the door with the side of his fist, he hollered her name until his throat hurt.

When no one answered, he stumbled back, slipping down the steps and landing on his butt with a thud. He ignored the pain, scrambling to his feet and staggering into the unkempt lawn.

The house felt empty. He knew in his heart that it would be.

Even so, desperate determination made him run to the tower. He climbed on shaky limbs, his feet slipping as he carelessly sped up the vines. The window was still wide open, never closed after Helena's heart-wrenching fall.

He slipped through easily and whispered her name. "Helena?"

All was quiet.

Creeping to the attic stairs, he strained for any noise that would indicate life, but he found none.

Tiptoeing through the empty *castle*, he checked every damn room until he could no longer deny reality.

She was gone.

And he had no idea where to find her.

Bile burned his throat as he wrenched the front door open and tripped onto the porch. He caught himself before falling and yanked the door closed. It slammed with a sickening finality.

She was gone.

He stumbled back to his place, looking like a drunken fool as he wove down the sidewalk in dazed confusion. He reached his house and fell against it. Slapping his hands onto the weatherboards, he let out a desperate yell and pounded the wood until his hands stung.

Gone! They took her without a word!

Did she fight to see him again? Did she cry?

He hated that he couldn't be there for her...to wipe away her tears, to hold her...to carry her.

"I can't carry her," he murmured.

The thought that he couldn't keep his promise was sickening and he bent down and suddenly threw up. The hot, sticky vomit stank of pain and misery.

"Tristan?" His father trotted down the back stairs,

worry marring his strong face. He ran over to him, his solid hand landing on his back. "Are you okay, buddy?"

"She's gone." Tristan didn't even recognize his voice. It was a thin, strained sound, barely audible to his thundering ears.

"Gone? What are you talking about?"

"They took her, Dad." Tristan sucked back a sob. "She wasn't there and the nurse can't tell me anything, and the house is empty. And she's...she's gone. Her family...from England. They took her," he screamed, hot breaths puffing out of him. "She's... How will I ever find her?"

It was like she was dead.

If he couldn't find her...

If he never saw her again...

He gulped in a mouthful of air, but it caught in his throat.

His coughing and hacking morphed into these weird-sounding sobs and he buckled against the house.

His father caught him, wrapping two solid arms around his body, and held him steady. Tristan pressed his quivering chin onto his father's shoulder and held tight, crying until he was nothing more than an empty shell.

With gentle murmurs, his father led him inside, blinking at tears of his own. Sitting Tristan at the table, he puttered around the kitchen while his son sat like an out-of-service robot on the verge of shutting down completely.

37

Shut Down Mode

It did shut him down.

Even when his father called the hospital and tried to demand a little more information, all Tristan could do was stare at the wall, a numb shell.

It was hopeless.

He didn't even know her grandparents' names. All he had was Cambridge, England. It wouldn't be enough—the search was too huge and there was no way of narrowing it down.

His only hope would be Helena contacting him, but

he had a sick feeling that she wouldn't be able to.

It was over.

He was never going to see her again.

He somehow made his way up to his room an hour later, stumbling inside and slapping his hands against the desk. He gripped the shiny surface, his chest and stomach aching from the crying. His eyes were swollen and tender. He rubbed at them anyway. His insides were raw and hollow.

Sucking in a ragged breath, he gazed out his window. The skeletal trees were in full bloom with spring blossoms, fresh new life reviving the trees to their summer splendor.

Tristan's eyebrows dipped and he lurched for the curtains, yanking them across and shutting out the cheerful view. Spinning around, he eyed the cranes dangling from his ceiling. His lips formed an ugly line, a bitter growl rumbling in his throat.

Jumping onto his bed, he snatched the cranes and yanked them off the ceiling, throwing them across the room and screaming, "Why?" until his voice was hoarse.

His bedroom door flung open and his father filled the gap. His face was etched with worry, his soft brown eyes brimming with compassion.

Tristan's knees buckled and he slumped onto his bed, bowing his head and sniffing.

"Leave me alone. Please," he whispered brokenly, "just leave me alone."

He closed his eyes, waiting in agony until the door finally clicked shut.

Gone.

She was gone.

He buried his head in his pillow, curling his body into a ball and closing his eyes against the paper cranes scattered on his bedroom floor. He willed oblivion to take him. He didn't know how else to manage the pain.

Four weeks passed.

Each day was long and painful, shrouded in anguish. Tristan didn't know how to cope with the world so he remained shut down, running on autopilot. Shuffling through the school hallways, he kept his head down and didn't really talk to anyone.

Miss Warren tried to hold him back after class but he ignored her request, dumping the poetry book on her desk with a bitter thank you.

That poem had become worthless. How could he carry Helena now? She was no longer part of his journey. It made everything pointless.

Squirming in his seat, he checked the clock on the wall and was relieved to see he had less than five minutes until he could get out of the hell pit and return to the sanctuary of his room. He barely opened the curtains anymore, enjoying the black haven he'd created. It was easy not to think in there, to simply sleep and pretend like nothing existed.

The bell trilled, a shrill sound that made Tristan jerk in his seat. A couple of students behind him snickered but he ignored them, snatching his books off the desk and walking out of the classroom while the teacher was still yelling instructions at him.

With his head down and his hands in his pockets, he dodged human traffic and made a beeline for his locker. Slowing to a stop, he spotted Mikayla's small feet planted on the linoleum floor and rolled his eyes.

She'd been talking to him every day, the only kid in the school who hadn't given up on him despite the fact that he'd stopped talking. Pressing his lips together, he rolled his shoulders and steeled himself.

Shuffling up to the shiny blue metal, he glanced at the back of her head. That's when he spotted the inside of her locker. His lips parted, a deep sympathy ripping through him.

Rotten bananas, black and oozing, covered all her stuff. He had no idea how they'd gotten into her locker, but it almost didn't matter. The damage had been well and truly done. Mikayla stood in paralytic shock, her petite nose wrinkled at the smell. Her chin trembled, her lips wobbling as she took in her ruined books.

Tristan knew who was responsible, but he doubted anyone could prove it.

He wanted to do something—tell her he'd kick Owen's ass, offer to go get the custodian, place a hand on her shoulder and tell her he was sorry—but he couldn't.

Instead he backed away from his locker, creeping out

of the school before she noticed him. Like a coward, he ran to his bike, unlocked it with shaking fingers, and took off for home.

Helena would have been so disappointed in him, but what did it matter? She wasn't around to confess to. She wasn't there to tell him what he should have done. She was gone and he was once again lost.

38

The Shoebox

Tristan pedaled as hard and as fast as he could, swerving around traffic and making it to Booth Street in record time. He took the corner too fast, nearly bailing on the hard concrete, but managed to pull the bike into line at the last second.

Puffing like a dinosaur, he stood and pumped the pedals, zipping down the street with his eyes on his letterbox.

But then a cat jumped out in front of him, darting onto the road without any care to human traffic.

Slamming on his brakes, the bike fishtailed to a stop, the front wheel clipping the curb. Tristan's bike wobbled and then buckled, sending him flying sideways. He smacked into the ground and rolled once, coming to land beside a tall fence. He hissed at the stinging graze on his knee, frowning at the newly acquired hole in his favorite pair of jeans.

"Shit," he muttered, pushing himself up and leaning against the fence to check his wound.

It wasn't too bad, just a little blood. Standing straight, he went to collect his bike and then noticed he was leaning against the fence surrounding the big green house.

The *castle* had been abandoned since Helena was taken away. Tristan had checked it daily for the first week and then given up. The constant disappointment was too painful.

Before he could stop himself, he peered between the cracks, eyeing the long, unruly grass, then flinching when he spotted a woman on the porch.

At first he thought it was the dragon, but when he squinted to really study her, he noticed the woman was someone else. She had the same blonde hair but was taller than Helena's mother, stood with her shoulders back, her chin held high. She carried herself with a confidence that Mrs. Thompson never could.

A new owner?

That couldn't be right, could it?

Before Tristan thought better of it, he shouldered open the gate.

The woman flinched, her blue eyes rounding with shock before narrowing with mild annoyance.

"Can I help you?" Her accent was posh and sweet, reminding him of Helena.

His heart spasmed and all he could do was frown at the foreign woman.

She cleared her throat and walked down the rickety steps. "Who are you?"

"Who are you?" he managed.

Her head jolted back. She was no doubt surprised by his rudeness. Stopping a few feet from him, she studied his face before her lips started to twitch with a smile.

"Your name wouldn't happen to be Tristan, would it?"

He wasn't sure how to respond. Who was the woman? And how did she know his name?

"Helena described you well." She extended her hand with a kind smile. "I'm her Aunt Sylvie."

"Helena," he whispered, snatching the woman's hand and shaking it like a lifeline. "Is she okay? Where is she? Can I see her?"

His questions were fast bullets, but she deflected them easily. Her expression crumpled with sadness. "She is as well as she can be...considering her condition."

"But where is she?"

"I can't tell you that."

"Yes, you can!"

She responded to his shout with a gentle sigh.

"I can only imagine how you must be feeling. Helena has cried many tears for you, but she can't see you again, Tristan. It's over."

His swallow was thick and audible.

"Her mother is in a very fragile state. We're getting her help, but at this stage she still blames you entirely for Helena's fall. We're in the middle of a very slow, hard, painful journey...and your presence will only hinder that. You must let her go."

"I can't," he croaked.

The woman's eyes glassed with tears before she blinked and brought them under control. Her keen blue gaze ran down his body, her eyes narrowing at the corners. "What happened to your knee?"

"Oh." He looked down at his torn pants and shrugged. "I just fell off my bike. I'm okay."

Her lips rose with a kind smile, her nose wrinkling like Helena's did.

He gazed down at himself again, his jaw working to the side before he nodded and said, "But she's...she's okay?"

"She'll get there. We're doing everything we can to help her heal."

"Will she walk again?" Tristan croaked.

The woman's expression crested with pain. "It's not looking likely. It doesn't help that her motivation is...well, nonexistent. She has a few bright moments, days where she seems stronger. But then I'll find her crying in her bed, not wanting to get up and face the day."

The soft words screamed volumes, making Tristan hurt in ways he didn't know he could.

"Please let me be there for her," he whispered.

"Even if I wanted to say yes to that, you know I can't.

I'm only here to box up the house and take back a few requested treasures. I'll be leaving in a couple of days...and you won't see any of us again." Her eyelids fluttered, her tongue peeking out to lick her bottom lip before she bit them together. She rested the back of her hand on her hip and looked away from him, squinting in the bright sunlight.

A bird chirped from one of the giant trees along the fence line, its wings fluttering as it shot into the air. Tristan followed its path, raising his hand to shade his eyes.

The sky was a brilliant blue, crystal clear with the promise of summer. Tristan hadn't even noticed how warm it had gotten or the brilliant green of the leaves in the trees.

Helena probably loved this time of year. She'd no doubt have something magical and poetic to say about such brilliant weather.

And whatever a sun will always sing is you.

Tristan's chest squeezed tight, his airways restricting as he remembered the poem he'd given her in the hospital. His hopes had been so high and electric in that moment.

Now they were gone...turned to ash that could so easily fly away in the breeze.

As much as he wanted to stay there arguing with the woman, he was logical enough to know it was pointless. His arguments carried as much weight as his ash-like hope.

It was time for him to go and put his bike away—time to go back into his darkened cave.

He pointed his thumb over his shoulder and started a backwards retreat. "Well, I should go and—"

"Wait," Sylvie blurted, surprising them both for a moment.

Tristan's forehead bunched.

She hesitated, obviously warring with some kind of indecision before giving in with a gentle sigh.

"I have something for you." She held up her hand. "Please, just stay there."

He did as he was told, watching the woman turn and disappear into the house. Biting the inside of his cheek, Tristan gazed at the crack in the pavement. Green shoots of grass were spurting between them—a splash of color on a dirty, gray canvas.

Tristan stared at the vibrancy of it, his vision going fuzzy as Helena's laughter tickled the back of his brain.

Here is the root of the root and the bud of the bud.

The poem came back to him line by line—a sweet, aching torture.

And this is the wonder that's keeping the stars apart.

Sylvie's steps on the porch pulled Tristan from his trance. He walked up the path to meet her. She stopped on the bottom step, clutching a shoebox to her chest.

His breath evaporated when he got near enough and she lowered the box. A white envelope was pinched beneath her thumb. *Tristan* was written on it in blue— Helena's swirling letters making it look far more regal than it deserved.

She swallowed, running her fingers lightly over the box.

"She wrote this for you on one of her better days, then changed her mind and tried to throw it away." Anguish washed over the woman's expression. "But you must read it." Her voice hitched. She cleared her throat and quickly regained her composure. "I was going to leave these on your doorstep before I left, but seeing your sad face and..." She sniffed. "I understand now why her feelings are so potent. She knows that letting you go is the right thing to do, but please understand that it's been very hard for her." She held out the box to him. "I found these in her attic as well, and thought...you might like them."

Tristan took the box and letter, his breath shallow.

She looked to the ground, uncertainty flashing over her expression. Closing her eyes, she let out a slow breath before raising her chin to pierce him with her blue gaze. "I wish I could give you a different story...a way to contact her...a promise. But it would be foolish to do any of those things. You must treat this letter as Helena's final goodbye. Please. Don't make this harder than it needs to be."

Tristan swallowed, suddenly wondering if he even had the courage to read it.

His lips quivered as he drew in a breath and whispered, "Thank you. I think."

She sighed, a sad smile cresting over her face.

The lump in Tristan's throat was so thick and impeding, he didn't know how he was supposed to say goodbye. Tears burned his eyes, threatening to fall. He locked his jaw against them, dropping his gaze to the crack in the concrete.

"Goodbye, Tristan," she whispered.

With a slow nod, he turned and shuffled down the path. The box felt heavy in his hands as he stopped on the curb. Snatching up his bike, he pushed it down his driveway, dropping it outside the garage before clutching the shoebox to his chest and racing up to his room.

39

The Letter

Closing the door with his butt, he flicked on his light and then fell to his knees beside the bed. Treating the envelope with a mixture of reverence and fear, he gently propped it against his pillow, saving it for last. First, he opened the box and gazed inside, a shaky smile forming on his lips.

It was filled with paper cranes, and resting on the top was a leather necklace. He pulled it out, running his thumb over the oval disk with the flying bird painted on it. His hand shook as he gently laid it on his rumpled covers and sniffed. He turned back to the box and gazed down at the mountain of cranes.

Reaching inside he pulled out one from the top, reading the script on the wings.

Tristan played my prince today. He was magical.

He grinned, reaching in for another.

We started writing a play—"Rapunzel's Rescue." Tristan has a bigger imagination than he thinks. I hope I can make him see it.

Tristan's eyes were a brilliant blue today. His uninhibited laughter is the sweetest music I've ever heard.

I had my first real kiss. Tristan's tongue is bewitching. He tastes like peppermint and I shall dream sweet tonight.

Tristan's arms around me make me feel like I can do anything. I'm not afraid when he is near.

Each crane made his heart swell a little bigger. It felt tight in his chest, like there wasn't enough room to take it all in. Crane after crane written for him. He'd filled her life with them, given her so much in such a short space of time, yet...

Yet she'd given it all back tenfold. She'd redefined him, and the second she was gone he'd retreated back into the shell he was in before he met her.

Guilt and despair wrestled for first place. Blinking hard, he wondered if he could cope with any more. But he gritted his teeth and snatched out his last crane before slamming the lid shut.

His breath iced over, a cold puff easing out between his lips as he read the words.

So this is what love feels like.
Tristan and Helena forever.

She'd sandwiched her words within a love heart and Tristan couldn't help a bittersweet grin. Tears stung as he brushed his thumb over the word *forever*.

"If only," he whispered.

Dropping the bird on his "read" pile, he glanced at the letter perched against his pillow. He had no idea what she wanted to tell him and he wasn't sure if he had the courage to read it, but his hand worked with a mind of its own, reaching for the envelope and tearing it open.

He pulled in a nervous breath as he unfolded the white sheet of paper. The writing was neat and flawless, and Tristan wondered how many times she'd composed the letter to get this final version.

He could picture her scribbling her thoughts, her long hair draped over her shoulder as she wrote to him.

Letting out a breath, Tristan held the paper lightly in his hands and began to read.

My dearest Tristan,

It is with deep sadness that I write, knowing we'll never see each other again. My heart is broken, yet in spite of this pain, I feel a sense of peace. It's a soft glowing light in the fog...and gives me the courage to tell you this...

No matter how much I may miss you, or how many nights I'll dream about our time together, and how many days I'll yearn to see you again...I now have the security of knowing that no matter what happens to my broken body, my heart will live on in you. I'll experience the world through your eyes, and that is what gives me hope.

I always thought the greatest love stories were fraught with tragedy, and maybe I'm right, but you've made me believe in fairytales too. You, the guardian of my heart, have been my dream come true.

I never saw you coming, and not once will I regret knowing you.

Now...as sole guardian, there are a few things I require of you. Things I shall never be able to do on my own.

This is an odd one to start with, but something I have always wished for. Get a tattoo. My mother will never allow it, and I can't see my grandparents capitulating either. I'm locked in a body that won't do as it's told, and if I'm honest, I don't know if I have the strength or will to learn to live with that. So, you must do this for me. Make sure it's not a silly one you'll regret after a year, but an epic one that's meaningful...something that represents us.

I also want you to start a bucket list. Things you must do before the end. I would like it to include:

~ Visiting castles that fairytales were born in. I want you to stand on the turrets and imagine yourself as king. Picture me by

your side, your ever-loving queen. Lavenders blue, lavenders green, remember?

~ Take me to Rome and Paris. Walk me through Sherwood Forest. Sail me down the Nile and then marvel at the pyramids. I want to see Petra, Victoria Falls, the Great Wall of China...the Taj Mahal.

~ Write me stories as you go. They can be real or pretend, I don't mind either, but I want to experience these places as if I were by your side. Make them good, so one day I might find them in a library or bookstore. I know you have it in you, Tristan. You could be a master storyteller. Don't hide yourself away. That would be a travesty.

You need to find the braveness inside you and cling to it. You are no longer the faint-hearted boy I met in the attic, but a knight—a defender of the weak. Men like that fight for justice and they protect those around them. Live up to your name and become the man you were destined to be.

Look for all the beauty and magic this world has to offer. Walk with your eyes and soul wide open and make every heartbeat count, so that you can give back and leave the biggest, brightest footprint this world has ever seen.

And lastly, this is something I really must insist upon...don't miss me. Instead, make me paper cranes and fly them into the sky. No matter where I am, my spirit will catch them, because wherever you go or whatever you're doing, I'll always be with you, oh keeper of my heart.

With all my love,
Helena

Tears scorched his eyes, winning the battle and trickling down his face as he folded the letter closed with trembling fingers. Gripping his mouth, Tristan swallowed, his jaw quivering. He couldn't believe she'd tried to throw it away; it would have been a tragic loss. He was grateful for Aunt Sylvie's intervention.

Holding his head in his hand, he covered his eyes and let out a disjointed whimper. He wasn't sure how to think or feel. Hope still battled with the shallow pain of knowing he'd never physically carry her again, never hold her or rewrite plays with her. Never sit beside her to read a book or smell her jasmine hair.

Opening the letter, he read the last few lines again. He didn't want to *not* miss her...but as he soaked in her words, he slowly came to the resolution that he didn't have to miss her, because she was there. She'd *always* be there.

Rubbing his chest, he willed his heart to beat with her song as he reread the letter twice more.

"I'll keep you with me," he whispered. "I'll never let you go."

Sucking in a breath, he sat back, sniffing loudly and swiping a finger beneath his nose.

"I won't let you down, Helena." He nodded, gripping the cover of his bed as determination fired through him. "You're going to live this life with me. I promise."

His heart swelled inside his chest as tendrils of hope weaved through his system, igniting, lighting, freeing him of the darkness.

Pushing himself up, he moved to the window and

flung his curtains open, drinking in the summer sunlight.

He pictured her bright smile as she tipped her head to the sky and closed her eyes, flinging her arms wide and basking in the warmth of the sun. There she was. He grinned, and she smiled within him. He could feel it.

"You're here," he whispered. "You're here."

40

The Ghost of Sunshine

Biking to school the next day somehow felt easier. Helena's letter sat in Tristan's pocket—a sheet of paper that he knew he'd carry with him daily for many years to come.

Parking his bike, he looked up at his school, a determined smile cresting within him. He could do this. He was *going* to enjoy the rest of his year, because he was taking Helena into the halls with him, and that's what she'd want him to do—enjoy, smile, capture those worthy moments in the day and write them down for her.

Waltzing along the corridor with a light step, he turned right and spotted Mikayla. She was pressed against her locker, Owen towering over her with his scathing laughter.

"And where do you think you're going?" he snarled.

Mikayla's little nose scrunched, her mouth dipping with a resigned frown.

Tristan's first instinct was to hang back and step up once Owen had left. He'd hug Mikayla, rub her back, and let her know that everything would be okay.

Helena would like that.

But knights fight for justice, her sweet voice whispered through him. *I want a better story than a comforting hug. Live up to your name, Tristan!*

The command electrocuted him into action.

"Hey!" He pointed at Owen. "Leave her alone."

Everyone in the hallway went still, their mouths dropping open with surprise.

The mute one spoke?

Tristan ignored the curious gaping and continued forward, training his eyes on Mikayla's aggressor.

He waited until he was standing less than a foot from him before speaking again. A righteous anger burned inside of him, fueling his words and tone.

"Enough with this intimidation bullshit. She doesn't want you. She doesn't want to talk to you, she doesn't want to hang out with you, and she definitely doesn't want to have sex with you! So you know what? From now on, you stay away from her. You don't look at her and you don't come near her."

Damn, that felt good to say!

His heart thundered with adrenaline as Owen's nose crinkled at the side, his lip rising at the corner. He looked like a bulldog.

Tristan stood his ground, ready to fight if he had to. The idea actually thrilled him just a little. It was a hell of a lot better than being a coward.

"This isn't your business." Owen's dark glare was an ominous warning.

Tristan fought the urge to spin and walk away. Instinct was warring with a dogged determination to be the person Helena wanted him to be. Clenching his jaw, he shifted his shoulders back and bunched his fists.

"Mikayla's my friend and you've made it my business by being an asshole. Now back off."

Tristan shoved Owen's shoulder, forcing him to move out of Mikayla's space. Owen lurched back and then raised his fist, ready for a fight.

"Mr. Stalwart!" Principal Smyth called from the end of the corridor.

Owen's skin blanched, his fist dropping to his side.

"Might I have a word in my office?" When Principal Smyth's left eyebrow arched like that, everyone knew he meant business.

Owen scowled at both of them, snatching his bag and shuffling through the crowd. As soon as the pair clipped away, a low murmur started in the corridor. Tristan saw a few fingers pointing his way but he turned his back on them, gazing down at Mikayla with a soft smile.

He couldn't remember the last time he'd felt so

triumphant. It was going to make for a great story.

"You okay?" He gripped the strap of his bag.

Mikayla's lips were still parted, her eyes round with wonder. Finally her face puckered and she tipped her head, sticking out her hand. "I'm sorry, I don't think we've met."

He snickered, a broad smile taking over his face.

"Is that a smile?" Her face lit with one of her own, her brown eyes dancing.

He shrugged, his grin still firmly locked in place.

Her eyes narrowed as she studied him. "You know, your eyes look really blue today."

He jolted at her words, thinking of Helena. Taking Mikayla's hand, he gave it a soft squeeze and whispered, "Thank you."

His earnest gratitude took her by surprise. He let go of her hand, his cheeks heating with color.

"What's up with you?" Her eyes narrowed.

He wasn't quite ready to tell her, so he shrugged and said, "I just feel happy, I guess."

"Happy? You obviously haven't looked in a mirror this morning."

He gave her a quizzical frown.

She chuckled, hugging her binder to her chest. "You look like you've been possessed by the ghost of sunshine or something."

He liked that...a lot.

Nodding with a small grin, he whispered, "Maybe I have."

Mikayla's nose crinkled. "Well, tell her to stick

around."

Tristan's insides sizzled as he reached for his locker. "Trust me, she's not going anywhere."

41

Transformation

Mikayla and Tristan walked to class together and even sat with each other for lunch. It felt weird to go from solo boy to having an instant buddy, but Mikayla was pretty cool. Her sense of humor was quirky and her down-to-earth, no-fuss nature was easy to be around. Tristan could see her becoming a good friend.

Tristan pulled out Helena's letter a few times throughout the day, rereading it during free period and again just before he biked home. He'd have it memorized in a few days, of that he was sure. It was nice having her voice in his head, and he'd already started thinking about how he was going to reply. He wanted to tell her that he'd fulfill those dreams...but he wanted to promise her something a little more too.

Skeletal dreams and wishes started to take shape in his mind, and he knew he'd cling to them until they became reality.

Turning onto Booth Street, Tristan cycled a little harder. Once again his tires squealed to a stop when he saw a taxi on the curb in front of Helena's castle. The trunk was open, the back door ajar.

He jumped off his bike just as Sylvie walked through the gate dragging a large suitcase behind her.

"You're leaving already?" He leaned his bike against the tall fence and ran to her side.

She passed the suitcase to the driver and gave Tristan a sad smile. "I have to get back."

"But you only just got here."

"I know." She nodded.

"Is everything okay?"

She nodded again but didn't say anything.

Tristan bit the inside of his cheek, resisting the urge to grab her shoulders and give them a shake.

Tell me the truth!

He wanted to yell at her, drop to his knees and beg her to take him to England too. But that would be futile.

Fighting frustration, he licked his lips and desperately tried to draw out the conversation. "What's going to happen to the house?"

"It's staying in the family for now. Beatrice can't face

the idea of selling it. The packers came this morning and boxed up most of their things. They'll be shipped to England, and there'll be no need for us to return."

"Oh." Tristan swallowed the painful lump in his throat.

Sliding his hand into his back pocket, he touched the letter, reminding himself not to fall apart. Helena was with him. Everything would be okay.

"Listen, I must go. I need to get to the airport in time for my flight." She stepped towards the cab.

Tristan reached for her arm before he could stop himself. "Wait!"

"I can't tell you where she is."

"I know. I just... Can you give me a minute. I want to write her a note."

Sylvie closed her eyes. "If my sister finds out..."

"Please. Just a note." He yanked off his backpack and scrambled inside for a pen.

Ripping out the last page of his English book, he used his teeth to uncap his pen and quickly scribbled a note.

Sweet Helena...my guiding light...

I don't have time to say everything I want, but you need to know that I'll carry your heart with the greatest care. I'll honor your requests and I won't let you down.

Just know that you carry my heart too. I don't even know when I gave it to you really. It could have been the day I met you. It could have been that time you rewrote Romeo and Juliet for me. Or maybe you took it in pieces...until the entire thing was yours.

All I can tell you is that I'm happy for you to look after it for me, but rest assured that a man can't live without his heart for too long, and he'll search the earth to find it again.

Never give up hope.

Forever yours,

Tristan

Folding the note in half, he passed it over with shaking hands, hoping Sylvie wouldn't read it and decide not to pass it along.

"Promise me you'll give it to her," he croaked.

She let out a wispy sigh as she tucked the note into her pocket. "All right."

Her nod was stiff, but her blue eyes told him she would.

"Thank you."

He swallowed, the lump in his throat feeling large and prickly.

"She'll be okay, Tristan. She's surrounded by people who love her."

He bobbed his head and stepped back to give the woman room to leave. Standing on the curb, he watched the taxi drive away until it'd turned off Booth Street and disappeared around the corner.

For a moment he felt completely empty, the soul-shattering darkness edging in and trying to remind of him of what he didn't have.

But then he pulled out the letter. Gently unfolding it, he leaned against the fence and slowly reread each word. Like savoring a decadent chocolate cake, he soaked in each line, reminding himself of everything he hadn't lost.

He was going to live an amazing life.

And whether he found his heart again or not, at least he knew he'd never be alone.

Tucking the letter back into his pocket, he collected his bike and headed for the house.

He had a story to write.

42

Hear My Soul Speak

Tristan stood in the new bastion of Hohenzollern Castle, gazing out at the glorious vista below. A forest, peppered with magnificent trees—all shades of green—stretched out before him. The late summer breeze was warm and inviting. He breathed it in, a sad, yet peaceful smile resting on his lips.

"This is amazing," he whispered to his heart. "Wish you were standing right here with me."

His heart did a double beat—Helena's way of letting him know she was...although he couldn't deny the deep sorrow resting within him that day.

For the last three years, he'd been working his ass off to save enough money to take a trip to Europe. He'd even found the courage to secure a loan from his mother and Curtis.

At twenty years of age, Tristan had finally taken a leap of faith and headed to England in search of his heart. He'd spent most of his trip in London and Cambridge, asking questions, following trails, and ultimately coming up empty-handed. He was due back home in two days, and after a frustrating six weeks away, decided to end his trip with the first thing on Helena's bucket list—visit castles that fairytales were born in.

Well, this German castle sure fit the bill. It was magical, and he could understand why Helena swooned over the fact that her parents met there. He could picture the scene so clearly, imagining himself as King Kenneth, gazing out at the breathtaking vista before turning to spot the woman of his dreams.

He glanced to his right and noticed a girl leaning against the stone wall, facing out to Stuttgart. He couldn't see her face, but his lips twitched at the way her short blonde hair ruffled in the breeze. She tucked the locks behind her ears in an attempt to control them. Her neck was long and swan-like, giving her a regal elegance.

He nearly started wondering what her face looked like, but was distracted by thoughts of his Helena.

He turned the other way and spied a group of Japanese tourists taking pictures. They giggled and held up their fingers in the peace sign, posing for the photo with cheesy grins.

Tristan smiled and turned back to his own view, although it was impeded by visions of Helena.

He thought of her golden locks, so long and beautiful. The images in his mind had not faded...probably because he'd worked so hard to keep them alive. He'd spent hours writing stories about her, describing every detail so it stayed crystal clear. The way her green eyes shone like emeralds...the long golden braid that would sit over her shoulder. She'd been his Rapunzel.

Clearing his throat, he rubbed the tattoo beneath his shirt, patting his chest with a soft smile.

I carry your heart with me had been inked onto his chest the day after he graduated high school. Mikayla had designed it for him, her artistic flair making the quote magical. The words were sandwiched between two stylized paper cranes.

His best friend had finally pried out the truth about his tower girl and she knew everything. She was actually the one who insisted he spend his summer searching England for her. She'd offered to come with him, but he wouldn't let her. She'd fallen in love in her second year of college, and he couldn't imagine her boyfriend being overly happy about her traveling the globe over their summer break.

He'd kind of wanted to come alone anyway. Even though he hadn't found Helena, it'd been a good trip...the first time he'd really stepped out on his own. He needed to know he could do it.

If he was one hundred percent honest, the whole

experience had been epic. As heart saddening as it was not to find his girl, the chase had been thrilling. Multiple stories had formed in his mind throughout the journey as he met amazing people, walked into village pubs that were hundreds of years old, and stood outside a grand home that once belonged to Helena's grandparents. He'd pictured her inside it, wondered which room she'd slept in.

Stories filled with beautiful maidens, evil queens and brave knights, through to tales of stuffy boarding schools, horrible headmistresses, and a brave girl in a wheelchair escaping out the back door grew in his mind. He'd been jotting down notes ever since.

Tugging a notebook from his back pocket, he flipped it open to the middle and scribbled down *German castle perfect setting for Rapunzel retell. These towers are epic.*

His lips twitched as another scene appeared to him. He could picture a sword fight on the bastion and turned to watch two knights battle it out in his mind. Licking his bottom lip, he let the scene play through, wondering if the story he was building should go that way. It would be an exciting element to the climax he had planned.

He was taking every writing and English class he could at college. It was really helping hone his skills and develop his passion for the written word. Helena had been right...he really did have it in him.

Pursing his lips, he recaptured the scene with an added twist.

"You know, you could use this old-school setting with modern-day characters," he murmured. "That could be cool."

His mind's eye changed the scene and he pictured two guys fighting it out on the stones: swords became fists and an epic hand-to-hand battle unfolded. A whole new story bloomed from that one thought, excitement skipping through him as he reopened his notebook and jotted down something new.

He grinned at his bullet point, laughing at himself for using paper and pen. He should be dictating into his phone, but he couldn't bring himself to do it. Helena would love his old-school style, and his notebook was already becoming a precious treasure. If he ever did find her, he wanted to hand it over and watch her face as she pored over the pages.

"Wish I could find you," he whispered. "I miss you every day."

Going for his right-hand pocket, he took out a paper crane. He'd become an expert folder; a stack of blank cranes was always at the ready. Leaning his notebook on the uneven stone, he scribbled on the crane's wings.

Standing in the place your parents met. It's magic, and stories are being born here. Can't wait to share them with you one day. Your forever hopeful Tristan.

Tucking his pen and notebook away, he held the crane in his fingers, tweaking the wing before launching it into the sky. The wind picked it up and spun it back over his shoulder, catching the bird and making it fly.

Tristan frowned as he watched it, surprised by the lift it was getting, like some spirit was controlling the airflow that day. The crane twirled and danced, shooting up and over the wall towards the carriage courtyard.

Tristan snickered and decided to follow it. He'd rather have his crane disintegrating in a tree than be read by some visitor on a castle tour. Working his way back around, he hurried to the courtyard and slowed to a stop when he spotted his crane on the ground...next to a wheelchair.

Long, elegant fingers clutched the metal rim of the wheels as the owner stared down at the crane.

Tristan's lips parted as his gaze traveled up her slender jean-clad legs to her pale pink sweater...and braid of golden hair...

Suddenly he forgot how to breathe.

Tipping her head like a sparrow's, she reached for the crane with trembling fingers.

His heart, *Helena's heart*, began to pound so hard and fast his chest hurt.

Her perfect lips parted, her green eyes growing wide as she read his note on the wings. She still hadn't glanced up to find him; her eyes were locked on the paper, her bottom lip quivering as she reread the words. It was like she couldn't make herself believe it.

Tristan could sense her fears and slowly stepped towards her, still fighting for air as he closed the three-year gap between them.

He was less than a foot from her when she glanced up with a gasp. Her eyes brimmed with tears that quickly fell.

Tristan crouched beside her wheelchair and brushed them away with a shaky thumb.

"*Hear my soul speak*," he whispered. "*The very instant I*

saw you, did my heart fly to your service."

She let out a breathy laugh and replied, "Don't you mean my heart?"

Before either of them could utter another word, she wrapped her arms around his shoulders and pulled him close. The arm of her chair dug into his stomach, but he wasn't moving for the world. Her fingers bunched his shirt as she softly cried against his shoulder.

"When I saw that crane come fluttering down, I wanted so badly to believe it, but didn't know if I could." Finally pulling away from him, she held his face, her gaze shimmering like fairy lights as she brushed her fingers down his cheek. "I promised myself I'd leave you alone. Even after your note, I convinced myself that you'd be better off without me. I knew the only way you'd ever find me was if fate played a hand."

Tristan's face buckled with confusion. "How could I ever be better off without you?"

She looked down at her paralyzed legs and shook her head. "I'm a burden."

Tristan leaned back and gazed down at her. Running his hand lightly over her thigh, he denied her claim with a simple smile. "Never. I will never see you that way."

Her eyes glistened and she gave him another trembling smile.

"Besides, look at you. You're here in this amazing castle. You're not letting life stop you from doing anything."

"I almost did, but I couldn't give up when I was carrying your heart. It's a big responsibility." She smiled.

"I knew I wanted to come here, but I lacked the courage. It's taken me a long time to realize that not being able walk doesn't make life impossible. And shutting myself off from the world wasn't making me feel better. Aunt Sylvie promised me she'd bring me here as soon as I was ready."

Glancing over my shoulder, she indicated with a little raise of her chin. Tristan whipped around and spotted Helena's aunt, her wide-eyed surprise almost comical.

Helena giggled behind him. "Now I know why it's taken me so long to come. Our hearts have been waiting for each other to be here."

Helena's words warmed Tristan from his head to his feet. He grinned at Sylvie and she gave him a delighted smile in return. Then he looked back at Helena, still in awe of the fact that she was sitting right in front of him.

She's real. I can touch her.

He took her hand and gently ran his thumb across her knuckles.

"I..." He didn't know what to say. Perfect words didn't exist inside this much-unexpected surprise.

"You're a man now." She grinned, tweaking his hair and smiling at him. "Even more handsome than you were before."

He gave her a shy smile while reaching for her braid. "You cut your hair?"

She blushed. "Just to my shoulders. I needed to do something drastic. Mother was horrified, of course. And in the end I missed it, so I've been growing it out again."

Tristan swallowed. "Your mother, is she...?"

"She's at home with my grandparents. They're looking after her for me." Helena's eyes dipped to the ground. "The truth is, I moved in with Aunt Sylvie's family last year. It's been difficult not to be plagued by guilt, but...I was suffocating. Grandpa and Nana have been very supportive, although it's still hard." She winced.

Tristan brushed his thumb over the frown lines on her forehead. "How's she doing?"

Helena shrugged. "She has her good and bad days. She's able to leave the house now but doesn't like to walk too far away. She can handle going into the village as long as one of us is with her." She licked her lips, a flash of guilt cresting over her face. "Me being this far away has been a slight setback, but hopefully not detrimental."

"It won't be," Tristan mumbled, not wanting to taint their precious reunion with worry or guilt.

Helena's eyebrows puckered before she slowly raised her eyes to look at his face again. Her gaze traveled from his eyes to his mouth, her lips twitching as she leaned forward and murmured, "My heart." Gripping his shirt, she pulled him so close he could feel her breath on his lips. "I don't care how hard I have to fight. I will *not* lose it again."

Her lips were a soft caress at first but as his arms gripped her waist, the kiss became something more. It was so familiar yet new. Her tongue was still sweet and delicate but captured his own in a way it never had before. Running his hand up her back, he lightly gripped the back of her neck and reveled in the beauty of Helena exactly where she belonged.

He didn't know what the future looked like anymore. And in that moment, it didn't even matter. He'd found his girl again. His heart was safely home...and like Helena, he'd fight to keep it that way.

Epilogue

The Boy Who Came Home

The printer on his desk buzzed and clicked while Tristan tapped his finger on his arm and paced his small office. He was nervous. He couldn't help it. He'd just finished his first-ever book and it was with a sick sense of dread and excitement that he was giving Helena the final chapter to read. She'd had input throughout most of the story, but he had wanted to keep the ending a surprise.

As much as she'd pestered him, he'd managed to stay strong...even on those nights when she laid beside him, whispering in his ear, her hot tongue trying to coax the story out of him. He hadn't caved, because he'd wanted to surprise her with the truth.

His head was filled with enough stories to keep him going for years... everything from wild fantasies to international spy espionage to one heart-wrenching tale about a lost love never found.

But the first story he'd completed was his own.

The printer went still and Tristan bit his cheek, squeezing his arm before uncrossing them and reaching for the pages.

Walking out of his study, he brushed past the hanging paper cranes adorning the corridor and glanced out the window of his little English cottage. He stopped to smile as he watched Helena pick a ripe lemon off the tree in their narrow backyard and sniff the yellow skin. She closed her eyes and smiled as she breathed in the citrus scent. Tristan adored how she made even the simplest pleasures so beautiful and compelling.

He'd moved to England a year ago, as soon as he'd graduated from Vermont College. His father had come with him to meet Helena's family and help the couple get set up in their new cottage. It was a gift from her family, paid for by an early inheritance. Her mother had moved in with Aunt Sylvie and her husband. They lived just down the road, which was both a blessing and a curse. Helena's mother had reluctantly accepted Tristan into her daughter's life but still popped over frequently to check in. Sylvie was working on their behalf to reduce the visits, and Tristan was applying every ounce of his patience to make sure they went as smoothly as possible.

At least she couldn't accuse him of not looking after her daughter. He'd become an expert on Helena's condition, and over the past year the couple had set up routines and systems that made their adjusted life as simple as it could be.

Thank God her family is away this weekend.

Tristan fought a grin as he headed out to the backyard. To help Tristan out, Sylvie had convinced her sister to head to Devon for a long-weekend break with their parents, and Tristan was taking full advantage of the uninterrupted time. His insides skittered with excitement as he thought about the evening ahead.

But first things first, man.

Clearing his throat, he stepped onto the porch, catching Helena's attention when he closed the glass door.

She flipped her hair over her shoulder as she turned to look at him. "Is it done?"

"It's done."

She let out a gleeful chuckle and wheeled over the flat grass.

He winced as he handed her the pages, praying she'd like them.

"Oh, take that look off your face. I'm going to love it." She winked, then started reading.

Tristan chewed his lip. Helena was currently studying literature at a university in Oxford, excelling in all her classes the way Tristan knew she would. It meant that her critique of his work was always brilliant, yet sometimes tempered by brutal honesty.

Sitting on the sofa they had moved outside so they could look at the stars at night, Tristan bobbed his knee while he waited for her to finish. It didn't take her long; the last chapter was brief and to the point.

Her face was radiant as she read his final words, then hugged the pages to her chest. "I love it."

"You love it?" He leaned forward, skimming his fingers through her hair. "Are you sure? You're not just saying that?"

"Tristan." She tipped her head and gave him an emphatic look. "It's perfect. The world is going to fall in love with Author Tristan A. Parker."

He cringed. "So you definitely think I should publish it, then?"

"I don't just think it, I know it." Her smile was kind as she met him halfway and kissed his lips. "You've come so far, my love. As have I. You've taught me to live in this world."

"And you found me a home in it."

Their eyes met and shone in unison for a moment. Tristan could have stayed locked there all night, drinking in her beautiful face as the day faded into dusk.

But Helena had more important things to do.

"I have a paper crane to write." She went to move away, but Tristan grabbed her chair before she could. Putting on the brake, he scooped her into his arms and fell back against the sofa, capturing her smile with his lips before she could argue.

She giggled into his mouth as he mumbled, "The crane can wait."

"Don't let me forget," she said between kisses.

He grinned. "Do I ever?"

She pressed her body against his before whispering, "No, but you always give me about three more before I can get to writing the one I intended."

"That's not a bad thing, baby." He palmed her back and deepened their kiss, his heart swelling in his chest as he thought about the engagement ring waiting for her inside the paper crane beneath her pillow.

The final words of his book echoed in the back of his mind, as he picked up his future fiancée and carried her to their bedroom...

Once upon a time there was boy who was lost...until one day he met a girl who showed him how to dream, how to love, and how to find his way home.

THE END

Thank you so much for reading Paper Cranes. I really hope you enjoyed it. If you'd like to support my work, please leave a review on Goodreads or Amazon. This validates the book and helps me reach new readers. Thanks for your support.

WHAT'S NEXT?

The Barlow Sisters Trilogy

Mystery and romance weave together in this set of fast-paced, sports romance novels.

Follow the Barlow sisters as they negotiate the perils of forbidden love while finding their place at a new school in the troubled town of Armitage.

Curve Ball (Book 1) is due for release September 2017.

To keep in touch with Jordan's next project, sign up for her newsletter...

http://www.subscribepage.com/u5u0a3

You'll receive an exclusive gift of the Nelson High Playbook—an inside guide to the characters in The Big Play Novels, plus a short story linked to The Brotherhood Trilogy.

AUTHOR'S NOTE

I've never really written anything like this before. I wanted *Paper Cranes* to have a very ethereal, fairytale quality to it, but still have realistic elements...like the reality of mental illness and how debilitating and heartbreaking it can be. And the impact divorce can have on children.

If I'm completely honest, the story started out very differently. In my original version, Helena died. You might wonder why I chose to take that path, but at first I thought Tristan's story had to be told that way. He was lost, and he needed someone to show him the way. Helena did just that. She showed him so much beauty in the short time he knew her, and it changed his life.

I loved the idea that Tristan was carrying Helena's heart with him. E. E. Cummings is pure genius. That poem is one of the most amazing things I've ever read. It's actually printed on my wall, and was the inspiration for this book.

But it didn't sit right with me that I was going to break readers' hearts. Writing the original version broke mine, and after a long discussion with my editor, I decided that I needed to give you a happily-ever-after, because that's what my books are about. I know life isn't perfect, far from it, but that's why we have fairytales and books...things to inspire us. If Helena can rewrite the ending of Romeo and Juliet, then I figured I could rewrite Tristan's story too. He still got to carry Helena's heart the way I wanted him to...but then he found her again...and that makes me very happy.

I hope you've enjoyed my first Fairytale Twists novel...and I hope you can find some of your own paper cranes to write.

Thank you so much to all the people who continue to bless my life—my readers, my editors, my cover designer, my proofreaders, my awesome Songbirds & Playmakers.

Thank you to my amazing family, who I am so incredibly grateful for.

And thank you to Jesus, who I carry in my heart—my daily inspiration and the constant love of my life.

xx

Jordan

JORDAN'S BOOKS

THE BIG PLAY NOVELS
The Playmaker
The Red Zone
The Handoff
Shoot The Gap

THE BROTHERHOOD TRILOGY
See No Evil
Speak No Evil
Hear No Evil

FAIRYTALE TWIST NOVELS
Paper Cranes

THE BARLOW SISTERS TRILOGY
Curve Ball
Strike Out
Foul Play

ABOUT THE AUTHOR

Jordan Ford is a New Zealand author who has spent her life traveling with her family, attending international schools, and growing up in a variety of cultures. Although it was sometimes hard shifting between schools and lifestyles, she doesn't regret it for a moment. Her experiences have enriched her life and given her amazing insights into the human race.

She believes that everyone has a back story...and that story is fundamental in how people cope and react to life around them. Telling stories that are filled with heart-felt emotion and realistic characters is an absolute passion of Jordan's. Since her earliest memories, she has been making up tales to entertain herself. It wasn't until she reached her teen years that she first considered writing one. A computer failure and lost files put a major glitch in her journey, and it took until she graduated university with a teaching degree before she took up the dream once more. Since then, she hasn't been able to stop.

"Writing high school romances brings me the greatest joy. My heart bubbles, my insides zing, and I am at my happiest when immersed in a great scene with characters who have become real to me."

CONNECT ONLINE

Jordan Ford loves to hear from her readers. Please feel free to contact her through any of the following means:

WEBSITE:
www.jordanfordbooks.com

FACEBOOK:
www.facebook.com/jordanfordbooks/

INSTAGRAM:
www.instagram.com/jordanfordbooks/

NEWSLETTER:
This is the best way to stay in touch with Jordan's work and have access to special giveaways and sales.
http://www.subscribepage.com/u5u0a3

COVINGTON PUBLIC LIBRARY
622 5TH STREET
COVINGTON, IN 47932-1137

Made in the USA
Columbia, SC
18 October 2017